NEW
HEIGHTS

The Author would like to thank;

My very patient editor and friend;
James R. Woestman

My brilliant support tech and friend;
Robert J. Hornickel

Molly at @We Got You Covered Book Design for doing
an amazing job on my formatting and cover design.

All my Beta Readers!

Professor Braulio Corral of Corral's Martial Arts for his
assistance.

My Precious Family

To my sweet Caleb and Cammie for your patience and
love, and cheering your mom on through this whole
crazy author journey. I love you so much!

SKY WALKER

NEW HEIGHTS

Cynthia L. McDaniel

NEW HEIGHTS

ISBN- 978-1-7325796-3-7

This book is lovingly dedicated to my parents Kenneth and Mary McDaniel. Thank you for blessing me with a home full of love and a life full of Christ. I love you both and miss you more than words can express.

"The air up there in the clouds is very pure and fine, bracing and delicious. And why shouldn't it be?—it is the same the angels breathe."

- Mark Twain -

ONE

THE POUNDING OF the mighty Black Hawk's blades popped over my head as I loosened my seatbelt and leaned over to get a better view outside, from the partially opened door. I had been flying regularly in helicopters over the last year and a half, and the thrill of it still never got old. Major Silva, my new boss for the last eight months, glanced over at me somewhat startled, and started to motion for me to sit back in my seat. I smiled as he stopped himself and smirked, shaking his head. I knew he was thinking, what I was thinking. What's the worst that could happen? I would fall out of the helicopter? That's not too big of a deal for a girl who can fly anyway. Yes, you heard me right and I'm not crazy. Thanks to an accident I had with a failed World War II experiment and being cut and contaminated with a mysterious pink formula, I can fly, and I mean fly as in Superman flying!

Instead, he gave me the cutthroat motion and glanced at the two Army pilots who were busy manning the flight operations in the front. I could read his thoughts through his eyes so well now. He didn't want me to do anything to risk them finding out. If I fell out that would be two more people who knew our little, top government secret about me. Two more people too many. As of right now, we were already up to 17+ people (that I know of), who knew about my flying power; my mom, my baby sister Kass, my best friend Alicia, my boyfriend (now Army Warrant Officer Johnny Angel), plus General Collins at Ft. Campbell, and the head staff at the research compound outside of Houston, where we were now enroute to.

Oh yes, not to mention the higher ups that I haven't even met yet.

The Black Hawk approached the large, bright blue lake that was a sign to me we would soon begin our descent to the research facility. This was my sixth trip to this Texas facility since I had revealed to Major Silva and the military of my flying superpower. That was over a year and a half ago, and I was now 19 years old and 9 months into my military career with the Air Force, a path I decided to take for the protection of not only myself, but my family also.

The bright April sun burned against the blue water, shooting prism beams of light against us, as the water began to swirl on our approach. I looked for the large dome and the space shuttle that sits majestically beside it, to appear over the horizon out of the endless miles of nothing in this deserted space. One lone road snaked its way through the dry green grass and red dirt, and I was surprised that anyone could find their way out here. This place was the epitome of "the middle of nowhere."

My stomach fluttered in anticipation of seeing my research crew, but it would be five whole days until I could leave. I was especially anxious to get this trip over with, because on Friday I would be flying out of Houston to Tampa, where I would be spending Springbreak with Johnny and his family. I hadn't seen Johnny since Christmas, as he was finishing up flight school at Ft. Rucker, to complete his helicopter pilot training. We have been dating for almost two years, and with everything being as crazy as it was, I had yet to meet his parents except for the occasional Facetime call.

The helicopter now safely hovered over the big red circle on the southside of the research dome. I looked down to see Chief Master Sergeant Bryant looking up waving. Every trip I had come, I could pretty much bet on him being here on the tarmac awaiting my arrival, despite his busy schedule as commander of the unit stationed here. He always greeted me with a hug, forfeiting the salute I respectfully owed him. He treated me like family and was one of the main reasons I looked forward to my quarterly evaluations here.

I double checked my crisp blue flight suit to make sure

I looked presentable. My long curly, dark hair was piled into a sleek low bun, that peeked out from under my helmet. I smiled and waved down at CMS Bryant.

"Is he here to meet you everytime, Claire?" Major Silva asked, smiling and shaking his head at me.

"Yes," I almost yelled above the chopping blades. "I think he still doesn't believe I'm for real."

Major Silva laughed, "I can relate."

The helicopter touched softly down and Major Silva and I thanked the two pilots who were busy powering down their systems. I couldn't help but wonder if the pilots questioned why they flew me out here four times a year. I've had these two numerous times.

I gathered my belongings and Major Silva and I disembarked the helicopter, bending down under the now slower moving blades as we made our way as quick as possible to CMS Bryant.

"Hello Claire!" CMS Brant yelled above the roar of the Black Hawk engine whining down.

"Hello Master Sergeant Bryant!" I smiled brightly as he gave me a one armed hug.

Major Silva stood at command and saluted CMS Bryant, who in return saluted back.

"At ease," CMS Bryant smiled as Major Silva shook his hand. "Did you have a good trip?" he asked as we grabbed our luggage.

"A little bumpy coming in, but you know how those military flights can be," Major Silva laughed.

We headed toward the large pristine white and

silver building that had at one time been so unknown and intimidating to me. CMS Bryant asked the same questions he asked every time we met. How was my new career in the Air Force going? How have I been feeling? Have I noticed any changes in my health and most importantly of all, has anyone else found out about my flying power? I was glad that so far, I could answer the last question with an honest "No Sir."

Keeping grounded was not an easy feat for me. I loved flying more than anything and despite being warned by the higher ups to stay out of the air, it was all I could do to keep gravity from leaving my body and rocketing towards the stratosphere.

CMS Bryant stopped just before entering the busy complex, afraid that someone may overhear our conversation inside.

"So this week is going to be pretty much like the last few," he informed us in a hushed voice, "however we are going to be spending a little more time in the dome. There are some flight exercises we want to test on you, Claire."

"Yes Sir," I smiled in appreciation. They both knew how much I loved the dome.

Inside, the reception desk stretched across the glossy two storied lobby. I grabbed my regular room key from Jenkins, the red-headed clerk I met my first time here.

"The usual?" she laughed handing me the key to room 1012. This room was the room my mom and I stayed in on our first trip here, and I had requested it ever since.

"Yes Ma'am," I smiled. "How are you Jenkins?"

"I'm fine. How about you? What do they have you coming out here for this time?"

I smiled politely at her, unsure of how to answer. Jenkins was very curious about me and asked each time I saw her what I was here for, but in not so many words.

"Oh you know, just the same old research stuff." I shrugged my shoulders. I was a terrible liar.

"You must be part of the new NASA research council," she pressed further.

Major Silva walked over quickly to us and put an arm around my shoulder.

"Jenkins, how are you?" he asked, reading her last name off her badge. "Airman Haley, we better get moving."

"See you later, Jenkins," I said, looking over my shoulder, as he skirted me off to the elevator.

Major Silva pushed the button for the tenth floor after we stepped inside. "Claire, try not to get yourself into conversations like that if you can help it," he lectured me after the door closed. "I know you were just being nice, but I'm afraid your quickness to trust people too soon may get you into trouble one day."

"Yes Sir," I said, a little embarrassed, though I didn't feel like that was completely my fault. Major Silva rarely scolded me, but lately I seemed to be getting myself into sticky situations without even trying. He was constantly reminding me to stay out of the sky, especially in the airspace over my hometown of Clarksville, Tennessee. I had been spotted a few times when I first started flying and the legend of the "Witch of Clarksville," had grown to a fever pitch lately.

The latest was just two weeks earlier. This is a story you just have to hear. Kass (my baby sister), Alicia (my best friend), Lexi (our closest friend who had no idea I could fly), and I had gone to an Aerosmith concert together. This was going to be our last hurrah before Lexi left to spend the summer in California, before starting her sophomore year at the University of Tennessee. It was also for her birthday. You have to understand, Lexi had wanted to see Aerosmith since she was a little girl and they had finally come to Nashville.

The Bridgestone Arena was bursting at the seams that night. I felt like I had walked into a 1980's MTV video. Guys rocked cut off, heavy metal band tee shirts, while the girls donned black fishnet stockings under blue jean cut off shorts...and the hair. There was hair everywhere, teased out to the max, specifically for this special night. The girls and I had put on our eighties best. Kass was an exact replica of Cyndi Lauper, while I rocked fluorescent everything and glitter in my high hair. Lexi looked like the 80's surfer chick she was and Alicia settled for a toned down version of Selena in honor of her hispanic heritage.

Aerosmith finally took the stage around 9 pm. Steven Tyler electrified the whole arena. We had seats just ten rows back from the mainstage, (compliments of my military status) and screamed when they hit the first bar of "Dude looks like a Lady," with us belting out the words like a champ.

After the concert, we did what any crazy girl fan would

do, and went around to the back of the arena in hopes of getting just one glimpse of the band. A small crowd of fans, who had the same idea we did, formed in front of a tightly locked, chain link fence.

"There's the bus!" Kass exclaimed.

"There's no way we're ever going to get in there," Lexi sighed. "They don't even pass by here to get to the bus."

"Maybe if we yell, they'll come over here," Alicia said, putting an arm around Lexi.

That's when I had, what I thought was a brilliant idea. I scanned the perimeter looking for a private place to fly over the gate. If I could get to the band, maybe they would stop over to see Lexi. At last I saw a safe way over. Across the parking lot on the opposite side, a large oak tree butted up against the fence that led to the side of the building.

"I'll be right back," I whispered to Alicia. Five minutes later, I was flying over the branches of the tall oak and landed safely in the shadows of the tree and the building. I inched my way to the only doors in sight. The only doors they could possibly exit, to get to the tour buses. I took a deep breath and entered a long hall stretched out before me.

"Alright Steven Tyler, where are you?" I whispered.

The sound of voices echoing down the hall caught my attention. I tiptoed toward the sound, turning the corner at the end and peeked around the door. To my delight I saw the whole band standing around, talking to a lot of other people, but obviously ready to leave with bags in hand. This was insane. Two years ago, I would have never had the courage to do anything like this, but flying had given me a boldness I had never had before.

I took a deep breath, trying to find the courage to enter, then felt a strong hand resting on my shoulder. "May I see your VIP pass, please?"

I looked up at the biggest, buffest security guard I had ever laid my eyes on.

My face immediately flushed a bright red. "Umm, I'm actually just here to see Steven," I said pointing behind me.

The security guard smirked at me. "Sorry sweetheart. That's not happening."

I sighed in disappointment.

"Hey, what you got there Louie?" Steven's gruff voice echoed behind me. I turned around to see him walking towards us and for a moment I could easily have passed out. "Hey there, darlin," he smiled at me.

Holy Cow. Was this even happening right now?

"Hi Mr. Tyler…" I said stuttering over my words and reaching out to shake his hand. "My name is…" Oh no. What's my name? "My name is Claire, and we…my sister and my best friend Alicia, brought our friend Lexi here and it's her birthday, and she's dying to meet you."

Steven was so gracious to me, gently moving his hand from mine that had been shaking his nonstop since I started talking. He said he would gladly stop to meet Lexi on his way out. I thanked him over and over again, then quickly texted the girls telling them to stay put.

Steven and his crew walked out with me, on their way to the buses. As soon as we walked through the doors, a loud roar came from behind the fence. The crowd that had been only a few dozen, had grown to at least 500 people. The outside security guard had found Kass, Alicia, and Lexi and brought them inside the gate. Lexi froze up, but still managed to get an autograph and pic and say a few words to Aerosmith.

Long story short, it was the best night ever except for one little thing. Someone in the crowd had taken a picture of the tour bus on their phone and had managed to get me flying down from the tree in the background. I was about 20 feet off the ground, so I wasn't too worried about it. I thought it basically looked like I was jumping, but anyway, it hit Steven Tyler's Insta fan page the next day and Major Silva was not at all happy about it.

I honestly tried, but seriously, how could they expect me to *never* fly? That was like asking a bird to stop flying, or better yet, a helicopter pilot from flying. I used that comparison many times with Johnny when he was lecturing me about flying and it shut him down pretty good. He gets it. Flying is addicting, no matter what it takes to get you into the sky.

Major Silva and I settled in and headed down to the cafeteria for dinner.

"Claire!" I heard Jacobson, one of my poker buddies,

call out from one of the tables by the salad bar. "When did you get in?"

"I'll be right back," I told Major Silva as he headed to the food line.

Major Silva looked back at me over his shoulder. "Remember what I told you."

"I got this, Sebastian," I teased, calling him by his first name.

"Hey you guys," I smiled as I approached him and a group of my late night poker buddies.

"Hey Haley," they all said in unison.

"When did you get in?" Jacobson asked again.

"Just a bit ago. I'm here until Friday."

"Awesome," he laughed. "Next time, give a guy a heads up."

Jacobson, who was a 6'4 blonde haired/blue eyed, former football player, was one of the few guys here that knew of my flying power. He worked in the dome, helping to track my speed and timing, while also guarding outside when needed. All the rest of the guys just assumed I was in special operations.

"I'm sorry," I apologized. "It was kind of a last minute plan. I'm going to meet Johnny in Tampa this weekend, so I had to get my quarterly in before I went."

"It's fine," Jacobson smiled. "I'm looking forward to some poker and dome time." He winked at me. Anyone around us would have thought he was flirting, but I knew what that wink was about. Jason Jacobson was just as excited to get into the dome as I was.

I made a plan for a poker game that night with the guys and then headed back to my table where Major Silva was already half way done with his dinner.

"Good grief," I laughed. "I can't believe you ate so fast."

"Well, you better eat fast too. We've gotta get you up to the fifth floor for your blood draw."

I cringed thinking about the dreaded blood work. Not so much for the pain of the needle, but the uncertainty of the outcome. I feared results time, and not because of what the flying potion could be doing to me, but instead that it would get weaker, thus making me no longer able to fly.

My only sense of comfort in that scenario was a secret only Johnny and I knew about. I still had the small tube of the pink "rocket juice" I had stolen from the airfield hangar the night I broke in. I had it hidden in a safety deposit box in Clarksville, but even that didn't feel like a safe enough place for it. I vowed to myself if I ever lost my ability to fly, I would immediately inject myself with it. I never want to live without my flying superpower and I could never imagine living a life of normalcy again.

TWO

AFTER DINNER I was escorted upstairs so Dr. York could get some blood samples drawn. During the accident, I had been cut by glass test tubes that contained the pink liquid that had given me the power to fly. He checked me every visit to see if the pink potion had changed my blood anymore than it already had. My first four visits here everything had been the same, but on my last visit, Dr. York had noticed "*heightened levels of the foreign matter*" in my blood type. In other words, "foreign matter" meant they still had no idea what the pink potion was made up of. I felt normal and my body was behaving normally, except now I could control when and how long gravity held my body to the ground. He was very curious to see how much had changed in the three months since my last visit.

The doors to the elevator dinged and I walked onto the glossy white fifth floor of the medical unit. I followed Major Silva past several occupied rooms. I didn't dare look inside as we walked by. I stared straight ahead. I was here for something unbelievable and top secret, so who knows why they were here. I don't know what I was thinking. Maybe they were aliens or something. Nothing would surprise me anymore.

The lab was the last door on the right and I laid back in my usual seat waiting for the nurse's poke. She took five vials and was closing up the last one when Dr. York came in.

"Ahhh Claire!" he said, patting me on the leg with a manilla folder that had my last name "Haley" on it. "How's my favorite patient?"

"Hey Dr. York. I bet you say that to all your patients," I teased.

Dr. York laughed. "No, you're definitely my favorite… and the most intriguing." He looked at the nurse. "Thank you, Brooke," he said, dismissing her from the room. She left immediately, closing the door. "How are you feeling?"

"I'm fine. Everything's pretty much the same."

Dr. York smiled and nodded. "I don't think you'd tell me anything was different, even if you thought you were dying."

I shrugged my shoulders, smiling. He was pretty much right.

He held out his hand. "Mind if I see your wrist, please?"

I held out my left wrist and he twisted it gently upright, softly rubbing his finger across the Saturn ring tattoo that had mysteriously appeared the day I found out I could fly.

"Any changes with it?" he asked, examining it closely.

"No Sir…" I paused and bit my lower lip. "Well, to be honest, the streaks in the rings have been glowing a much brighter pink lately," I lowered my voice, "when I'm flying."

He stopped and looked up at me. "Does it hurt?"

"Not at all."

"Hmmm." He looked back down at the tat. "So after the accident, this appeared within 24 hours, correct?"

"Yes Sir," I replied.

"And you've never seen it glow as bright? Not even the first night you realized you could fly?"

"No Sir, I mean it was bright enough to light up a good section of the pool I landed in, but nothing as vibrant as it is now."

"How do you hide the glow?"

"Well, makeup works pretty well, but it's not always glowing. Only when I'm flying or thinking about flying."

"And how often is that?"

"All the time," I smiled mischievously.

Dr. York nodded, smiling back. "I figured. Well Claire, I'm going to be honest with you. I'm not sure, and I will know more this week, but I feel like this foreign blood type is not going anywhere soon. I've been studying your blood tests since the last quarter and the "Oc" blood type actually seems to have grown more dominant."

"Is that a bad thing?" I asked nervously.

"No...well, you seem to be fine and I don't want you to worry, but it's certainly something we need to watch."

I stared down at my tat and nodded my head slowly.

"Claire, you're in good hands here. My job is to make sure you stay healthy through all of this and that's what I'm going to do." He paused for a moment. "You know, a blood transfusion could be a possibility. We talked about that already."

I looked at him and shook my head no. "With all due respect, no thanks Dr. York."

"Well, we'll cross that bridge when we get to it," he reassured me. "We'll figure it out, Claire."

I slowly got up from the chair, the exhaustion from my 5 a.m. wake up call hitting me all at once.

"I'll get going on this in the lab, so we can start running tests and get as many answers as we can before you leave on Friday," Dr. York said, helping me up the rest of the way from my chair. "Are you ok?"

I stretched my arms high above my head, letting out a slow yawn. "Yes Sir, I'm just tired from traveling."

"Well, get a good night's sleep, because you have a busy day tomorrow."

"I will," I replied, remembering my poker game I had scheduled for later. I would definitely have to reschedule. I was way too tired. "Thank you, Dr. York."

THREE

"THANKS FOR BLOWING us off last night," Jacobson said the next morning as we walked to the dome after breakfast.

"I'm sorry," I laughed, yawning at the same time. "I'm just so tired, Jacobson. I've been going for two weeks straight."

"Well, flying isn't going to help. You're usually pretty well spent after you fly."

"I know," I yawned again, pulling my long brown curls into a messy bun as we walked, "but I'm so excited to fly. Major Silva has really been on me about staying out of the air. Back in Clarksville, there's a rumor going around about witch sightings and he's afraid they're going to tie it all together with me and start asking questions."

"Wait a sec," he said pausing in the middle of the

flower lined sidewalk. "You mean people have seen you flying and they think you're a witch?!"

"No, people *think* they've seen a witch," I winked at him. "No one has anything concrete on me."

"Oh Claire, you better watch that," he warned.

"I know," I agreed as we approached the dome. I paused as he scanned his name tag to open the door and we walked inside. The vacuum of air being sucked in from the outside slammed the door closed behind us.

Once inside, Jacobson turned and scanned his name tag across the lock and we heard a bolt snap into place.

Major Silva was waiting in one of the offices that lined the side of the wall. He smiled when he saw us. "Good Morning, CMS Bryant is running a little late, so Claire you get changed and I'll meet you in the dome as soon as he gets here."

"Yes Sir," I answered and headed down to the locker room.

Thirty minutes later I was suited up in my blue NASA jumpsuit, and Jacobson and I sat patiently waiting on a bench under the ten story high dome. Jacobson was holding my left arm, staring intently at the tat on my wrist.

"So you fell on a crate that contained the flying potion and you sliced your wrist open?" he asked, rubbing his finger across the Saturn rings.

"Yep. The pink potion got inside of it, into my bloodstream, and the next thing I knew I could fly," I explained.

"So this showed up where the cut was? I- I'm sorry for all the questions, Claire. I just always wondered what happened to you."

"I honestly don't mind the questions," I laughed. "Yes, my cut was gone overnight and the tat was in its place."

"Well, what does it mean?"

"I have no idea. I wish I did," I lowered my voice. "and I wish somebody here knew. I know they're trying, but it's been almost two years and I still have no answers."

Jacobson looked up at me. "Maybe there are no answers, Claire."

That stopped me in my tracks. My mouth gaped slightly open and I stared intently at him. That had never even crossed my mind. I had complete and total trust in Dr. York, CMS Bryant, and most of all, NASA. I knew somehow they would figure all of this out.

"This is no ordinary case, Claire," he continued. "I wouldn't have believed you could fly, if I hadn't seen it for myself. It's going to take some time to figure you out."

"I know," I sighed. "But I thought with the journals Major Kearney left behind, they could at least figure some of it out."

CMS Bryant and Major Silva interrupted our conversation and to my surprise Dr. York had joined us as well. We stood at attention as they approached, saluting on cue. The men saluted us back and we began to follow them to the staging area for testing, where Commander Whitley was waiting. Commander Whitley was in charge of running all the tests on me. He was a former flight instructor with NASA, and had a barrage of items waiting for me to be tested with. He drove all the way from Houston to be with me every week I was here. I immediately noticed his new NASA flight suit.

"Hey Commander Whitley. Nice suit," I teased.

"Don't worry Claire," he laughed. "I have one with your name on it."

CMS Bryant looked over at us. "Jacobson, I want you to do a general patrol of the area. Again, make sure the doors are secure and no one else is in the building.

Maize is the only one who should be around and he is patrolling the outside. When we know everything is secure, we'll get started."

"Yes Sir," Jacobson saluted and turned away, giving me a quick wink.

He had told me this morning he hoped he would be on patrol inside instead of outside. He loved to watch me fly.

I smiled back at him as he scurried away, then turned my attention to the gentlemen.

"Claire," Major Silva said, "Dr. York is here to get some vitals on you during your flight."

Dr. York nodded his head in agreement and began strapping a monitor on my arm. "I'm going to see how your heart is responding to a sudden change in gravity pressure, and also to monitor the rings again."

I looked down at my Saturn rings that were glowing with specs of pink, in anticipation of flying. I had mentioned to Dr. York that the rings glowed only when

I was in flight or extremely happy. I didn't mention the fact that they glowed the most when I was with my Johnny. (I'm supposed to be a strong soldier. I didn't want these guys thinking I'm a total mushball.)

"Ok Claire," Commander Whitley said. "We're going to start with weights. Last month you did good with fifty pounds. Let's add ten more and work our way up from there."

Dr. York wrapped a blood pressure monitor around my arm and I waited patiently as he listened to my heart.

"Is it ok?" I asked way too soon. He held up one finger requesting silence a moment longer and moved the stethoscope closer to my heart. I breathed in deeper on his command and after a minute he finally let go.

"Everything's good to go," he smiled down at me.

I breathed a sigh of relief, thanked him, and joined Commander Whitley in the center white circle, on the rubber floor of the dome. He began strapping weights on my arms and legs, as I looked up at the vast ceiling ten stories above me. The room was the size of a football field and housed various flight simulators and machines. I had no idea what purpose they served, nor did I dare to ask. Too much secrecy at this facility.

"Alright Claire, let's do this," Commander Whitley said, tightening the last weight.

Major Silva turned and looked at the door where Jacobson was standing guard.

"Are we a go Jacobson?" he yelled across the dome.

"We're good!" he yelled back, giving two thumbs up.

"Alright Claire, let's go up about 15 feet and hold it there," Commander Whitley instructed me.

Flying for me was as simple as walking. All I had to do was think about it and my body did the rest. I bent my knees and pushed my body into the air, effortlessly. The weights made flying a little more work against my body but it was no different than carrying the weight while I was walking. Plus, what my muscles lacked in stamina, my adrenaline definitely made up for.

Pausing at 15 feet, I looked down on the awe filled faces staring up at me. No matter how many times they watched, they always looked as though they were seeing me fly for the first time.

"Okay Claire," Commander Whitley yelled up at me. "How are they feeling?"

"They're ok," I yelled back down to him. "I can feel them pushing against me, but it's no different than if I were walking."

"Alright," he replied looking down at this clipboard writing my information down.

I waited patiently for him to instruct me further. At last he looked up. "Go ahead and fly up for a couple of minutes and then come back down."

He didn't have to tell me twice. I looked up at the red, white, and blue dome ceiling, and set my sights on one of the sun lights that cast a bright white spotlight through the ceiling onto the floor below. I shot through the air coming to a stop at the sunroof. I pressed my hand gently against the glass, and looked up at the cloud filled, sunny sky wishing I could go further. It had been a while since I had been flying, and while flying in the dome was nice, it was nothing compared to rocketing through a warm star filled night. My body craved flying. I don't know if it was the potions effect on me, but it had almost become a necessity in my life.

I flew around the dome, concentrating on the weights gravitational pull on me. I started feeling their resistance and my body grew tired under the strain, but in no way was I going to let the guys know that. Have you ever had to carry around 60 pounds for ten minutes? It was not easy. After about ten minutes, I heard the bullhorn sound, my signal to come down. I looked down at all their faces looking up at me and decided to shake things up a little.

I stood straight up, lifting my hands in the air, pressing them against the ceiling of the dome. I posed as though I was diving off a diving board.

"Bombs away!" I said to myself as I thrust my body into the air, lining it up in perfect diving form, head first.

"Claire!!" I heard Major Silva yelling at me through the bullhorn.

I plunged even faster than I thought I would, as my body adjusted to the new weight. The dome floor sped closer and closer and for a moment, I thought I wasn't going to stop. 100 feet, 80 feet, 50 feet, and finally at 20 feet, I flipped my body to feet first, and came to a sudden halt a mere 10 feet above the rubber based floor.

"Claire!" Major Silva almost yelled at me again. I

slowly floated the rest of the way down into the middle of the circle of men, who were now scowling at me.

Oops. Apparently that was a big mistake. I did it at home all the time, not realizing how terrifying it must look. My eyes looked past the scowling faces in search of Jacobson who had turned three shades of white, but was smiling in awe and giving me a quick thumbs up. I turned my attention again to Major Silva, who was wiping his brow with a handkerchief. He spoke a little calmer. "You have to stop with the craziness until we can get this whole thing figured out."

I started to argue my point with him, something along the lines of, *I do this all the time,* or *I know my own body.* But I decided it wouldn't be too smart arguing with my superiors or letting them know diving from the sky was the norm for me.

"I'm sorry," I whispered, looking at their eyes that were piercing me. "I promise it won't happen again, Sirs."

Dr. York approached me cautiously, "Well, I need to get your blood pressure, but after that I'm not sure how accurate it will be."

"I'm fine. Seriously, Dr. York."

"We'll see about that," he said, wrapping the blood pressure gauge around my arm. It squeezed tight and I felt my tattoo get hot under the pressure. "How were the weights? Are you sore anywhere?"

"Not really," I said. "I mean, it's the same as me carrying 60 pounds on the ground. But I'm totally fine," I reassured him.

Dr. York placed the stethoscope on my chest and listened for a moment. "Well, everything's good on my end," he said, turning to CMS Bryant. "Her vitals are normal."

I breathed a sigh of relief, especially after the stunt I just pulled. Major Silva must have read my thoughts, because he shot me a warning look.

"That doesn't mean you have the go ahead to pull stunts off like that, Claire," he warned me.

"Yes Sir, Major Silva," I cringed as he smiled back at me.

FOUR

I SPENT ALL morning in the dome flying, taking breaks as my body needed them. From what I was figuring out, I could pretty much carry in flight what I could carry if I were walking.

After lunch, Commander Whitley, CMS Bryant, Major Silva, and I sat alone in folding chairs, in the middle of the dome and discussed everything from heights that I had flown, to Commander Whitley's previous days as an astronaut (which I had no previous knowledge of). He was such a fascinating man.

Commander Whitley again warned me of the dangers of flying and I listened to him intently.

"You know, Claire," he said. "I know and understand the thrill and love of flying. Flying in a space shuttle is an out of body experience, so I can only imagine what you are experiencing and the addiction that comes with it." He looked at me more seriously. "But, I just want to remind you of the dangers you can face, and I'm not just talking about the potion wearing off." He paused for a moment, tapping his pen on his ever present notebook, that had my last name 'Haley' scrawled across the top of it. "Have you ever felt light headed?" he asked. I shook my head no. "You know at 1,500 ft. you can lose consciousness due to lack of oxygen and fall right out of the sky?"

"Commander Whitley, I think the highest I've gone up is 700 feet," I said trying to ease his mind.

He nodded his head. "And of course you know better than to fly in a thunderstorm."

"Of course."

CMS Bryant chimed in. "Claire, there is so much to consider when it comes to you and your safety. I hesitate to bring this up, but we want to be honest with you so you are aware of the responsibility that comes with this power that you have."

I cocked my head sideways looking at him, not knowing exactly what he was getting at.

"We have other countries spying on us all the time. Ummm...if...if they found out about you, we worry that you would become a target for them. A real life human Superwoman is something any government would love to add to their arsenal of knowledge."

"You mean, as in someone possibly kidnapping me?" I asked in disbelief.

"Perhaps," CMS Bryant said swallowing hard. "Nothing's off the table Claire...and I'm not trying to frighten you...well, in a way I am. I just want you to be aware of what is around you, and what we, as government leaders, face with protecting you."

Major Silva chimed in, his southern Spanish accent extra thick today. "Which is why it is so important that no one finds out. Enough civilians around you know already and we are going to do everything we can to protect you."

Everyone was awkwardly quiet as I sat and pondered all they were saying to me. I heard the familiar warnings of someone seeing me, or getting caught in a thunderstorm, but never had I ever given thought to someone kidnapping me.

"What would happen if I were to be seen flying?" I finally asked.

"Well, we would take you into hiding, probably in a facility like this that is heavily guarded...and try to do a lot of damage control." CMS Bryant responded. "And I think I know you well enough to say you definitely are too much of a free bird for that."

I nodded my head in agreement. How horrible would that be? There was no way I could ever be stuck in one place. Not ever.

"So what you're saying is no flying ever," I sighed.

"For right now," Commander Whitley replied, frowning slightly. I could tell he sympathized with me. "I know this is a heavy statement Claire, but this has become a matter of National Security. The bigger guys are really staying on all of us about you."

"Who are the bigger guys?" I asked.

"You'll know when the time is right," CMS Bryant said, patting my shoulder as he stood up. "Well, I need to get to a staff meeting. Whitley, maybe 20 more minutes and let's call it a day."

"Yes Sir," Commander Whitley said as we all stood up to salute his departure.

Jacobson held the punching bag for me Thursday night, as I practiced my newly acquired kickboxing techniques in the spacious, modern gym that took up the whole basement floor of the building. Bruce Springsteen's "*Born in the USA*" blared from the speakers that shook the rafters, while weights clanked loudly and men who looked like they could easily fill the role of a Rambo movie, lifted around me. Jacobson had mentioned one time that there was a "special underground" unit that trained here. When I pressed him for further information on them, he politely cut me off telling me that just because I can fly doesn't mean I have the right to know everything.

"Come on, Claire. A little quicker, remember to put your whole focus and energy on your leg. Throw a little more power behind those kicks. Use your hips!" he ordered me.

I wiped the sweat off my brow, balled up my fists, focusing on the outline of an assailant painted on the tall bag. I set my sights on the head and took a deep breath. Spinning my body around as fast as I could, I snapped my leg high into the air as straight as possible. Months of training had afforded me unlimited flexibility and the top of my foot landed squarely in the center of the face. I grunted loudly on impact.

Jacobson stepped backwards and I smiled to myself, knowing I had thrown him off balance.

"Well, that's a little better," he offered.

I shook my head in disbelief catching my breath. "A little better?" I argued with him, putting my hands on my hips. "It was enough to knock you backwards."

"I'm just sayin' Claire," he laughed. "If you're going to knock someone out, you have to do better than just knocking them backwards. Now come on. Hit me again. Kick through the target!"

I scowled at Jacobson, irritated at his lack of appreciation for my efforts. I spent the last 18 months trying to prove that my value to the military was far more than an accidental superpower. I wanted to matter and do all I could to contribute to my country.

I took a deep breath, focusing my energy on my kicking leg and with everything I had in me, turned and kicked the face on the bag. A loud smack rang out above the grunting and weight noise. I even left the ground and had to catch my balance as I found my footing again on the floor. Jacobson let go of the bag on impact and was knocked back several feet. He looked at me astonished, while the guys around us began to cheer and clap, teasing him for not being able to hold onto the bag.

"Good job, Claire," he smiled. "I have hope for you yet."

"So what time do you leave tomorrow?" Jacobson asked as he walked me to my room.

"I have to be on the tarmac by 8 a.m. sharp," I answered as we exited the elevator on my floor. "My flight for Tampa leaves at 11."

"Are you excited? You're going to get some beachtime."

I took the room key out of my pocket as we approached the door. "I am excited for that, because I've never been to the ocean. But I'm even more excited to see Johnny."

Jacobson leaned into my door, inching closer as I slid the key into the lock.

"Claire, please be careful out there. I... I worry about you." He looked down at the ground avoiding eye contact with me. "You mean a lot to me and I don't know what I'd do if anything ever happened to you."

I looked up at him, a little off put by the tone of his voice. He moved even closer to me than before and I suddenly felt a lump in my throat. Johnny was my first boyfriend ever, so when it comes to guys I could be a little naive, but it was pretty clear what Jacobson was getting at.

I twisted the bottom of my tank top, like I always did when I was nervous. I bit my lip unsure of what to say to him.

Jacobson slowly moved his hand to my face to remove a curl that was starting to fall from my high ponytail and into my eye.

"Jacobson…" My nervous voice croaked out.

"Jason," he said, smiling down at me.

"Jason," I repeated after him. "I appreciate your concern, but I'm going to be really careful. Ummm… besides, Major Silva has Johnny on me constantly, so I know I won't be getting much fly time anyway. He takes pretty good care of me."

I watched as his eyes slightly saddened, a sign to me that he got the hint. He took a deep breath and backed slowly away.

"I'll be here in the morning to help you with your luggage to the tarmac," he frowned slightly. "Good night, Claire."

"Good night Jacob…Jason." I smiled trying to make him feel better.

He laughed slightly and walked down the long hallway to the elevator. I slid my key in the lock and headed quickly into my room, then locked the door, leaning back against it. I felt bad, but was also feeling a little startled. I had no idea he was feeling anything more than friendship for me. Again, my lack of guy experience showing.

A loud rapping on the door made me jump, feeling like someone had punched me in the stomach.

"Claire, it's me," Major Silva called from outside the door.

I opened the door and he walked in, dressed in his civvies and smelling like a spicy cigar. He must have just come from a poker game with the higher ups.

"Hello Sebastian," I smirked. "Did you win big?"

"I don't play for money, Claire. I told you that."

I looked at him skeptically. "How much did you lose?"

Major Silva looked shamefully at the ground. "$132."

I tried, a little too late to cover my mouth, but a giggle came slipping out. I patted him on the shoulder. "Well, at least you don't have a wife to answer to. It's your money."

"Yeah, the only great advantage of being single," he said sarcastically.

I shut the door behind him. "What's up?"

"Well, I know we leave tomorrow, but since you're going to Tampa instead of back home to Ft. Campbell, I wanted to talk to you about a few things that came up this week."

"Ok," I said as we sat down on my little sofa.

"I just wanted to make sure that you're feeling ok with everything. I know we laid it on pretty thick, but I don't want you to worry about all of this. More importantly, I don't want it to interfere with your decision for a military career."

I shrugged it off not wanting Major Silva to know how worried I actually was. The whole "spy thing" had my mind spinning the last couple of days, and it had nothing to do with my safety, but the safety of my family. Just my younger sister Kass, who was going to be a senior in high school, and my sweet little mom were at home now. My dad had died when I was little, and my two older sisters lived away from Tennessee.

"I just want my family to be safe, Sebastian."

"Claire, you know we've got that covered. I would never let anything happen to them."

I nodded, relieved to hear him say that to me again. He assured me so many times they would be ok, but I always needed to hear it once more.

I placed my hand on his. "Which is why I know everything is going to be ok. I trust you."

Jacobson knocked at exactly 7:45 the next morning. I grabbed my duffle bag and placed it by the door, taking a deep breath before opening it. I didn't know how he would act towards me after the awkward conversation we had last night, but he smiled broadly at me as if nothing had ever happened. I was so grateful for that. I hate having an "elephant in the room." If I'm feeling something, I just have to say it right away. If I'm feeling uncomfortable in a situation, I have to clear the air about it. Holding stuff inside of me affects me physically, emotionally, and mentally. Plus I'm just really impatient and I don't like to have tension with anybody.

"Wow, those are some nice civvies," Jacobson said,

looking me up and down.

I looked down at myself. I had thrown on my favorite pair of comfy jeans and a somewhat dressy crocheted sleeveless shirt with my Birkenstocks. I didn't realize Jacobson had never seen me in anything but my flight suit and PT (physical training) clothes.

"Thanks," I smiled as he grabbed my bag.

We walked to the tarmac together where Major Silva and CMS Bryant waited for us. I could hear the roar of the Blackhawk's engine warming up as we headed down the flowered path and rounded the corner of the dome.

"So, I'll see you in a few months?" Jacobson asked loudly as we got closer.

"Yes. August," I smiled at him.

"Keep in touch Claire, ok?"

"Of course," I said, grabbing my bag and turning toward the helicopter, but then stopped and looked at him one last time. "Hey Jacobson, take some poker lessons," I laughed.

"You got it," he smiled, seeming a little more cheerful than before. "Enjoy my fifty bucks."

"Oh, I will!" I winked.

I joined CMS Bryant and Major Silva who seemed to be discussing the Blackhawk, but turned their attention to me as I approached.

"You ready to fly?" Major Silva smiled slyly at me.

"Yes Sir!" I answered in anticipation of the helicopter ride to the airport. I turned to CMS Bryant. "Thank you Sir for the helicopter and well, everything you've done for me."

"You're welcome Claire," he replied, giving me one of his fatherly hugs. I really liked CMS Bryant. He had become like a father figure to me. I could tell that he was genuinely concerned for my safety and worried about me. "Claire, please remember what we talked about," he reminded me. "Stay out of the sky, unless absolutely necessary."

"I promise, Sir." I said, telling myself in my mind I would definitely listen to him this time.

FIVE

I LOOKED OUT of the plane window as my flight from Houston to Tampa flew over the Gulf of Mexico. We were high above the clouds and I gazed at them in awe, wishing I was flying myself to Tampa instead of taking an airplane. Of course, I would have had to fly at night and I had never flown that distance before. Flying over the ocean had been a dream of mine for a long time and I secretly decided while I was there, I was going to make that happen.

The pilot glided the Boeing 747 smoothly onto the runway and my heart fluttered in anticipation of seeing Johnny. It had been four long months and I told my best friend Alicia that I likened it to going without a drink of water for that long. She rolled her eyes and once again reminded me of how dramatic I could be at times. I somewhat agree with her, but still, she had yet to go that long without seeing Shawn. Shawn was her boyfriend, and also best friend and roommate to my Johnny.

I grabbed my luggage and walked onto the ramp from the plane. An amazing, salty ocean smell immediately enveloped me and I paused on the ramp to breathe it in and pull myself together before I saw Johnny. Passengers scurried around me and I waited until the flow of traffic slowed down, then walked toward the gate. I rounded the corner and saw him immediately.

Johnny stood tall and distinct in the crowd of people. His tan popped against his feather gray Army tee shirt and black cargo shorts. His dark hair seemed a lot longer, for normal Army standards, and of course those emerald green eyes. You could see them from a mile away.

His face lit up when he saw me and for the first time I noticed a bouquet of bright pink roses by his side. Was this guy real? Even more than that, was he really mine? I'm pretty sure I carry the title of "luckiest girl in the world."

I ran the rest of the way to him and dropped my bag onto the floor, jumping into his strong arms. He wrapped them around my waist and pulled me close, slightly lifting me off the ground and squeezing me for a long moment. He then slowly set me on the ground, sealing it with a kiss. Normally, I'm not a PDA person, but in that moment, I didn't care. When he let go I pulled him back in, oblivious to the hundreds of people around us, until a few people oohed and awed as they walked by.

At last I let go and he smiled down at me. "This is never happening again, Miss Haley. Four months is way too long. I can't do it again."

"Same for me Mr. Angel," I agreed. "Never again."

"You ready?" He handed me the flowers and picked my bag up off the floor.

"Yes!" I said as he took my hand.

A half an hour later, we were heading south on Interstate 75 to Anna Maria Island, where his family lived. Johnny and I talked about our four months apart and how my week at the compound went.

"Johnny, I can't believe you're a Warrant Officer now!" I bragged on him. "I'm so proud of you."

"Thank you sweetness," he smiled so big, blushing slightly. I loved complimenting him. He was such a great person and a hard worker. His dream of becoming a helicopter pilot was so close now and I was really proud of him.

"Look at you, Airman First Class Haley. My girl is moving up the ranks."

This time I was the one blushing. "Thanks Mister." He was so sweet to me. I still couldn't believe this was my life. I had the most perfect boyfriend, an incredible career, not to mention I was the closest thing you get to being a superhero on this planet. What a crazy ride it had been so far for this Tennessee girl.

The sun shone warmly through the sunroof in his truck and I looked as the ocean spread far out to the west of us.

"So what do you think of the ocean?" Johnny asked, snapping my attention from the blue green water.

"It's one of the most beautiful things I've ever seen," I said in awe. I had never been far outside of my hometown of Clarksville, Tennessee, much less to the ocean, when all of this craziness went down. Now I could add Florida to Texas on my list of states visited.

"I'm going to take you sailing this week, so you can get a real taste of it," Johnny said, squeezing my hand a little tighter.

"You know how to sail?" I asked, surprised. I knew he was a competitive windsurfer, but I had no idea he could sail too.

"Of course. I grew up on the ocean, Claire. You learn to ride a bike, you learn to sail."

We crossed a bridge that led us over an ocean canal to the island. My palms grew sweaty and my tummy turned in anticipation of meeting his family. Would they like me? Would they think I was smart and pretty and good enough for Johnny? I hated my self doubt and thought I had pretty much left that behind with my flying power and the confidence it gave me, but here it was again, rearing its ugly head and filling my mind.

Johnny turned his truck down a hidden driveway, and through the brush and palm trees a large three story Mediterranean home came into view. I had never seen a house like this before. It was so beautiful. Just beyond it, waves were breaking on the beach that lay at the end of their plush green lawn.

"Your garage is the bottom floor?" I asked.

"Hurricane protection," Johnny laughed.

"It's beautiful, Johnny."

"Thank you," Johnny smiled at me. "My great grandfather built a house here originally, but it was destroyed by a hurricane in 1921, so my grandfather built this one higher. It was the first of its kind on the island."

"I can't imagine what it must have been like to grow up here."

"It was pretty great," he said, turning off the car and grabbing my hand. I gulped hard and he laughed at me. "Nervous?"

"Yes," I cringed. "I hope they like me."

"Claire, they already like you. All you have left to do is meet them."

Johnny kissed my hand that he was holding. "You ready?"

I took a deep breath. "Yes."

Johnny's family was more amazing than I could have imagined. His mom, Nora, who was a petite blonde, and his dad Mario, a tall Italian man, immediately bear hugged me, making me feel right at home. Janey, his older sister, also a blonde, who looked like she stepped off the pages of a Pacific Sun catalog, and her fiance, Josh, welcomed me with a beautiful island bouquet to set up in my room while I was there.

"Claire, we are so thrilled you're finally here," Nora said that night while we ate by Tiki lights on the spacious deck of their home.

"Yeah, I don't think John would have made it one more day," Josh laughed, as Janey lightly jabbed him in the side.

I looked over at Johnny who was shaking his head and smiling at Josh.

"Thank you, Mrs. Angel," I smiled. "I'm so glad to finally be here."

"So how was Houston?" Mr. Angel asked. "Johnny said you were there for some kind of training."

I side glanced at Johnny. He knew I was a bad liar.

"It was for basic flight stuff, right Claire?" Johnny quickly asked. He always knew how to dig me out of sticky situations.

"Yes," I smiled. "We just went over basic gravitational flight procedures...umm that test our flight endurance... and our flight fatigue, stuff..." I trailed off. "*Shut up, Claire,*" I told myself, biting my lip to keep from gabbing on.

They all stared at me for a moment.

"Well, that certainly sounds interesting," Nora smiled graciously at me.

"What's your job description in the army, Claire?" Janey asked.

"Well, I'm actually in the Air Force," I explained. "Ft. Campbell has a small Air Force installation and they allowed me to train there."

Nora's eyes lit up. "I bet your mom is grateful for that."

"She is," I laughed.

"And so am I," said Johnny putting his hand on my knee.

"That's a really cool tat you have," Josh said, pointing at my wrist.

"Thanks."

"What is that? Space rings?" he asked.

"It's the rings of Saturn. I'm...I'm a space fan."

Josh leaned over the table to get a better look. "What kind of ink is that? It's almost like a pink neon/glitter color."

Johnny gently grabbed my wrist. "You guys haven't seen this kind of ink yet? It glows in the dark when the light hits it a certain way."

"I've never heard of it. That's really pretty, Claire," Janey said looking on the side of her arm at her cross tattoo that had a green vine wrapped around it. "I could add some of those pink flowers with that ink to my vines. It would pop even more."

"Definitely," I agreed with her.

"So what do you kids have planned for the week?" Mario asked, taking a sip of his water.

"Well, I was thinking about taking Claire sailing and then maybe hitting Disney one day."

My eyes grew big and I gasped. Disney World. I had dreamed of going to Disney since I was a little girl. When I was 8, my family was planning a trip to Disney and were just two weeks shy of leaving, when my dad passed away suddenly. That vacation was put away and never brought up again.

Johnny chuckled at me. "Claire, have you ever been to Disney?"

I suddenly felt a little embarrassed at my five year old reaction. "Actually no, but I've always wanted to go"

"Well, we're going for sure." Johnny said, squeezing my knee under the table.

The next evening I stood on the dock watching Johnny busy himself with getting the sail boat ready. The sun hung heavy in the afternoon sky and bright colors of purple and orange glowed on the Gulf Coast water. The waves splashed calmly against the dock and I wondered how we were going to go anywhere in a sailboat with no wind.

"Are you ready?" he asked, smiling up at me and reaching for my hand.

I took his hand and stepped cautiously into the boat. "Johnny, how do you sail with no wind?"

"This boat has a motor back up," he said, lifting me gently into the boat. "Don't worry, Claire. I've been sailing since I could walk."

"Oh, I trust you. I'm not scared. I'm too excited to be scared."

Johnny leaned down and kissed me on the forehead.

"Let's do it," he said, grabbing the rope to untie the boat and push us away from the dock.

Ten minutes later we were headed west away from the island with nothing but open waters ahead of us. Three miles off the coast Johnny killed the engine and set the sails so the wind pushed us further out. I sat at the bow of the boat watching the water skim quickly underneath us, occasionally reaching over the side and feeling the rush of warm salty water move up my arm. My navy blue summer dress blew in the wind and I was glad I wore my bikini under it, just in case we decided to jump in. 311's "Amber" blared from the boat speakers. I felt so light and free and knew sailing would become a must have in my life.

"Claire!" Johnny yelled from the helm. I turned and saw him pointing to the north. Three dolphins swam close, occasionally jumping out of the water as if they were racing with us. I got so excited, I jumped up on the bow to get a better look.

"Oh my goodness, Johnny! Dolphins!!" I yelled.

He smiled so big at me, obviously pleased at how excited I was. I turned back quickly to look at the dolphins and felt a sudden strong gust of wind push against my back. In an instant my footing slipped and the next thing I knew I was tumbling over the short rail, hitting the water head first. I heard Johnny scream my name and then nothing but the sound of salty water muffeling his voice as the current sucked me under with a vengeance. I kicked and pushed back, fighting with all my might to swim to the surface, but the more I pushed, the more I panicked and was losing what little air I had in my lungs.

Meanwhile, Johnny who was in a panic of his own, flew into action to slow down the sail boat and put it in motor mode, so he could turn around and find me. His hands shook nervously as he stumbled over the lines, quickly pulling down the sail, and starting the engine.

Underneath the salty water I struggled to find which way was up. My body twisted and twirled and was pulled further in the current.

"Come on, Claire. Fly!" I thought to myself. I didn't even know if I could fly.

I had never flown out of water before, and even still I had no idea which way was up. In a last ditch effort, I pushed my body upward to what I thought was the surface as darkness enveloped me and I slowly lost consciousness.

SIX

JOHNNY TURNED THE boat around attempting to get back to me as quickly as he could.

"Claire!" he yelled for me. "Claire!"

He later told me what happened next, he would remember for the rest of his life.

Johnny leaned over the bow of the boat desperately searching the water and calling my name. The waves grew stronger with each gust of wind. Suddenly, I rose out of the water 20 feet from where the boat was. My body was limp and Johnny said I laid straight on my back, unconscious, my legs and arms dangling, as I was suspended in the air at about 25 feet.

"Oh my God," Johnny gasped, trying to catch his breath, his eyes wide, staring at me for a long moment. "Claire!! Claire!!!" he yelled trying to wake me.

He pulled the boat close to me and dropped the anchor, then headed to the radio to call for help. Johnny stopped with the radio in his hand, pausing after he looked up at me again, realizing he couldn't call for help. He couldn't let my secret be known. I had shared with him what CMS Bryant said about me becoming a target for other countries and I could tell it really frightened him.

"Over my dead body, Claire." he had told me.

Johnny grew desperate and began to search the boat for some way to get up to me. He found a long blue ski rope and tied his coffee mug to the end, hoping to throw it up and somehow pull me in.

"Claire!" he yelled again and again, as he swung the rope with the mug as far as he could into the air in hopes of getting it to wrap around me. With each throw he grew more and more frustrated, as each one came within just a few feet of making it over me.

Up in the air, I slowly began to regain consciousness, looking straight up into the dark purple sky that was now turning a dark navy blue. I gasped for air and began coughing uncontrollably as a salty burning liquid came up my throat.

"Claire!" I heard Johnny's voice yelling at me.

I sat up and looked down at the ocean water and sailboat below me. My mouth salivated and I began throwing up more salt water than I knew my body could contain. When the vomiting finally subsided, I wiped my mouth and looked down at Johnny, feeling dizzy and confused. Suddenly, it felt like the sky dropped from beneath me and I plunged into the chilly Gulf waters.

Johnny dove into the water after me. He quickly swam over and wrapped his arms around my waist. "Hold on," he said, swimming back to the boat.

We reached the ladder and Johnny slowly followed behind, guiding me up and catching my waist when I lost my footing. I was exhausted. At last we collapsed on the floor, catching our breath. Johnny crawled over to me, wiping my hair out of my eyes.

"I'm so sorry," I said, coughing up more water. "I'm so stupid."

Johnny smiled. "No you're not, Claire. You didn't know. I'm just so mad at myself for not putting a life jacket on you."

I looked up at his worried face. "I'm a superhero. I'm not supposed to need a life jacket."

Johnny laughed, kissing my forehead and pulling me close to him. "I'm so glad you're ok, Miss Superhero. You were stuck up there and I had no idea what to do. I couldn't call for help for obvious reasons and I had no way to get to you."

I turned over on my side and faced him, trying to remember how I ended up in the air. "Johnny, I have no idea how I got up there. I just remember swimming and telling myself to fly out and that was it. Everything went black."

"You told yourself to fly out?" he asked.

"Yes, but I didn't know which way to fly. It was so dark."

Johnny's eyes lit up. "Well, that's it then!"

"What's it?" I asked, sitting up beside him.

"Your body was able to do what you needed it to do, without you being in control mentally."

I looked at him skeptically. "What do you mean?"

"Your body was on autopilot while you were unconscious," he explained. "Don't you see, Claire? It did what you needed it to do even though your brain was unable to send your body the right signals."

Oh wow. I definitely got it. "Almost like the fly potion kicks in when I can't control myself. And how did my body know to stop and not go further into the air?"

"I don't know," Johnny said standing up and taking my hand. He lifted me gently off the floor. "But we should definitely give Dr. York a call tomorrow and let him know what happened, just in case." Johnny walked me to the back of the boat and pulled a life jacket from underneath the seat. "Here, put this on. I'm going to get you back home before it gets too dark."

Johnny tightened the straps, then grabbed his sweat shirt and wrapped it around me.

"Johnny, I'm so sorry," I said, taking both of his hands in mine. "I feel like I make your life so much harder than it has to be."

Johnny laughed lightly. "Claire, you definitely make life more exciting." He took my face in his hands and kissed me softly. "I wouldn't trade you and all your craziness for anyone in the whole world."

The next morning I was on the phone with Dr. York for over an hour as I explained to him everything that happened the day before. He was as lost and baffled as Johnny and I were.

"Well Claire, if anything seems off, even the slightest little thing, please let me know and I will put a call into Major Silva and let him know. I swear, we learn something new with this potion almost every month. I just thought your flying power was a mind control thing."

"I thought so too," I agreed with him.

"I don't understand how you came out of the water when you were unconscious. It's almost like the potion has a mind of its own." Dr. York was talking to me, but I could tell he was more so, questioning himself.

"I know, Dr. York. I don't understand it either. But please," I pleaded with him, "don't let my mom know. She worries about me so much and I don't want to put more on her plate."

"Well Claire, you're 19 now," Dr. York reassured me. "You're the only one that can release any of your medical information, but I'll make sure to mention it to Major Silva in case he talks to her."

"Thank you, Dr. York," I said, hanging up with him.

Johnny sat down beside me on the bed. "You ok?"

"Yes, I just knew he would have no answers," I sighed, turning to him. "Do you know what Jacobson said to me that I never thought of before?"

Johnny shook his head no.

"Jacobson said maybe there are no answers and...and there may never be any answers." I looked at Johnny, with worry and frustration consuming my eyes. "I just never thought about that. I mean, people are working on my case who put big shuttles into space. I thought, if they can do that, then they can figure me out."

Johnny looked at me for a long moment. "I don't know Claire...if they don't have all the answers it's not the end of the world, as long as you're ok. Besides, you're not a space shuttle, you're a human being with a lot of human complexities to figure out." He smiled at me mischievously. "And you're a female on top of that. Even the smartest males in the world have yet to figure out women."

I lightly punched him in the arm, laughing. "Seriously? I'm around men twenty four seven and I've never seen such complicated creatures. You guys are drama kings and *EVERYTHING* is a big deal...oh, and God forbid any of you get sick. That pretty much equals the end of the world."

"Oh yeah?" Johnny smiled. "You wanna see some drama?" Oh no. I knew that look. "Here comes the drama tickle bugs!" he said as he pinned me to the bed in an instant.

"Johnny, no!" I screamed, laughing at the same time. I hated the tickle bugs!

Johnny sat lightly on my tummy, turning his fingers

into bugs that crawled all over me tickling me until I could barely breathe.

"Oh my God! Stop Johnny!" I laughed even harder, trying to grab his fingers and put an end to the torture.

"Come on, Claire," Johnny warned, laughing with me. "You know if you smash them, you're gonna get bit."

Johnny's right hand tickle bug climbed up my shoulder and onto the most sensitive part of my neck. I laughed even harder trying to push the tickle bug away to no avail.

"Don't smash it!" Johnny warned me again.

"Ok! I'm sorry!" I screamed.

"You mean you're sorry you said men are drama kings?" he asked, grabbing both of my hands in one hand and pinning them to the bed.

I paused for a moment, not wanting to apologize for what I said. "Ummm no," I laughed.

"Take it back, Claire," Johnny laughed.

"No way," I thought to myself. I looked at him as seriously as I could. "Johnny, I'd rather die a thousand tickle bug deaths than take back what I said about men." I tried my best to say it with a straight face, but immediately giggled at what I knew was coming.

"Ok, stubborn," he laughed, pulling the tickle bugs back out. I squirmed and endured a few more minutes of torture before he finally rolled off and laid on the bed beside of me. "I don't think I've ever met anyone as stubborn as you, or as ticklish for that matter," he laughed. "You know, you almost kneed me where the sun doesn't shine."

"Well, you would have deserved it," I laughed. "You and your tickle bugs."

Johnny sat up on his elbow and leaned over me. "Claire, seriously though, everything's going to be ok. I don't want you to worry anymore. I'm beside you no matter what."

"I know," I smiled up at him. "And that's the only reason why I'm ok with everything."

SEVEN

THE NEXT FEW days in Florida with Johnny were storybook perfect. He took me to Disney and we spent as much time out on the sailboat as we possibly could. Despite the fiasco from the first night, I had fallen in love with sailing.

On my last night there, Johnny and I packed a picnic and headed out on the boat to watch the sunset over the Gulf. At Johnny's request, I reluctantly donned the life vest as we were enroute, with the promise of being able to take it off as soon as we dropped anchor.

The evening was so perfectly beautiful. The wind blew lightly across the Gulf water, as seagulls flew overhead and the sun cast a perfect orange glow on the constant rippling water. The air was thick and smelled of salty water and fresh clean air. Johnny anchored the boat a few miles off shore and as soon as we stopped, my life jacket came off.

I watched as he spread out the red plaid picnic blanket on the small deck at the bow of the boat. Johnny looked so perfect in his blue beach shorts and white tank top, almost matching my white sundress and navy blue bikini.

I sat beside him on the deck as he unloaded the dinner we had made. His mom's fresh homemade bread tasted so perfect as we sat and talked about the past four months apart and how our summer schedules would match up. I was pretty excited when Johnny confirmed he would be back at Campbell, close to me. We knew there was a good chance with his promotion to Army Warrant Officer, he could be assigned to another base.

"What about Shawn? Is he coming back to Campbell too?" I asked.

Johnny suddenly became a little nervous, and fidgeted with the container the bread had been packed in.

"Johnny?" I asked, unsure if he had heard me or not.

Johnny's attention snapped back to me and I watched as he tried to recollect his thoughts. "Shawn?" he said, trying to catch up. "Yeah, Shawn's coming back too."

I looked at him curiously. "I know Alicia's relieved to know that."

Johnny nodded in agreement with me. His roommate Shawn, and my best friend Alicia, have been dating as long as we have.

"Are you ok?" I asked.

"Yes…" he said, biting his lower lip. "Actually, Claire,

there's something I want to talk to you about."

My heart dropped as the worst thoughts I could have possibly imagined flooded my mind, and the worst one of all; *"He's gonna break up with you, Claire. You're too much of a problem for him."* I knew that since I had met Johnny, his normal life had been turned upside down by my flying power. I had kept it from him as long as I could and that caused a lot of trouble in our relationship. We vowed to never keep secrets again, so what he was about to say to me had my heart racing. I said nothing, but fidgeted with the bottom of my sundress, like I always did when I was nervous.

Johnny noticed my nervous habit immediately. "Claire, stop fidgeting," he smiled. "It's not bad."

I smiled back at him, a little relieved, but still nervous. "I'm sorry."

"So I bought you something while I was training." Johnny leaned over me and grabbed a small tackle box off the bench. "I...I just thought we should make things a little more official."

My face is what my dad had called a "mirror to my soul." Anyone who looks at me, can pretty much tell what I'm thinking, and despite Johnny's best efforts to assure me everything was ok, I was a mess on the inside and it showed all over my face.

Johnny took my hand and started playing with my fingers. He was just as nervous as I was. "So, I'm only telling you this because Shawn told me I could....but he's going to ask Alicia to marry him this summer." (I tried to act surprised when he told me, but Alicia and I had pretty much already figured that out. Girls are pretty smart that way, plus Shawn was like me. Captain Obvious.) Johnny continued to play with my fingers, entwining his into mine. "So...I don't know, it just made me think about you and I. Claire, I don't know if you realize how happy you've made me, but I can't remember how I was ever happy before you. I mean, when I'm not with you, I'm counting the minutes until I can be with you again...and training these past few months was torture. I wanted to text you at least every hour, and I...I worried about you. A lot." Johnny placed the back of his hand gently on my face and rubbed my cheek. "I don't know what I'd do if anything ever happened to you."

Oh wow. I didn't know where he was going with this, but I bit my lip trying not to tear up. That was the sweetest thing I'd ever heard.

Johnny reached down and opened the tackle box. He pulled out a small navy blue ring box with a tiny pink bow on it.

"I know we've both talked about how unique our situation is right now, so I know you're not ready for a huge commitment, but I at least want you to know how committed I am to us."

He gently opened the box. I looked down at the prettiest ring I had ever seen in my life. A shiny round sapphire sparkled brightly, surrounded by tiny star-like diamonds, all wrapped up in a silver band.

"I thought it looked like the night sky. I know how

much you love flying."

As much as I tried to hold it in, tears flooded my eyes and rolled down my cheeks at his thoughtfulness.

Johnny laughed lightly and pulled me in close. "Awww Clairey, don't cry."

I wiped my tears, trying to pull myself together. "Johnny, this is the most thoughtful thing anyone has ever done for me. It's a…?"

"A promise ring," he finished my sentence for me. "I figured just because we're not engaged, doesn't mean we can't take the next step."

"It's perfect," I gasped, as he took it out of the box and put it on my left ring finger. I held it back and looked at its perfect fit. It was so beautiful. "Everything is so perfect. The picnic, the ring," I put my hand softly against his cheek, "and you. I'm so lucky to have you. I love you."

Johnny wrapped his arms around my waist and pulled me close to him, softly kissing me. "I love you too, Claire. So much."

I snuggled up beside him and we laid back against the giant pillow to watch as the sun slowly settled on the top of the water.

My thoughts shot back to a conversation we had the week before he left for flight school. We both agreed to take things slowly and that any talk of marriage would have to be put off until I could work out all the bugs with my flying thing I had going on. But secretly on my side of things, and of course I would never say this to Johnny, was the underlying fear of being married to him and then something happening to me. I was only two years into this ordeal and I thought about his future and how selfish it would be for me to marry him, not knowing if I would even be alive 5 years down the road to enjoy it. Sometimes I think it would be better for him to meet a normal girl, who he could have a normal life with, and not worry about all the craziness my life was wrapped up in. There were so many unanswered questions, like...could we even have kids? And if so, what were the chances of them turning out like me? Johnny never talked about the negative side of it, but I thought about it a lot.

That night I lay in bed wide awake, listening to the waves crash and roll against the beach. It was one of the most beautiful sounds I had ever heard. Johnny was so blessed. I couldn't imagine falling asleep to this every night. The bright moon glowed through the few clouds that skimmed the sky, shining down through the tall windows and casting a beam that hit on my ring. It shot speckles of light onto the nightstand beside me. I looked at the clock. It was 1:15 am.

From underneath the cover, my tat glowed a brilliant pink, my body almost pleading for me to take flight. Hmmm...I had always wondered what it would be like to fly over the ocean.

It didn't take much to convince myself and I slid out of bed and grabbed my Air Force duffle bag. Stuffed underneath the covers, it was a dead ringer for my 5'3", 117 pound frame. I crept over to the window, careful not to wake Johnny who was sleeping in the room across the hall. I slipped on my chucks and slowly cranked open the window. The humid salty air draped over my skin and blew my curls into my face. I grabbed my scrunchie and piled my hair into a messy bun high on top of my head, not caring that I was only in my jammie shorts and cami. The ocean water shimmered white in the bright reflection of the moon. I stood on the window sill and slipped outside into the open air, hovering while gently closing the window. Satisfied that it was secure enough for me to get back in, I dove backwards into the open sky, then flipped onto my tummy, and rocketed into the moist gulf air. Rising high above the sandy shore of Anna Maria Island, I gasped at the beauty of the lit up shoreline. Just to the north I could see the Sunshine Skyway, a beautiful lit up bridge that crossed Tampa Bay. I grabbed my phone and pulled up my playlist. One Republic's "Good Life" began pumping through my phone. I began recording, knowing it wouldn't be enough to just tell Kass and Alicia about this little adventure. They would want to see it.

"OK you guys," I narrated. "It's one in the morning here and Johnny is back at the house sleeping, but I knew you guys would want to come along on this little flying adventure with me tonight." I turned the camera toward the north. "So you see that bridge over there? That's the Sunshine Skyway that leads to Tampa. And this is the coast of Anna Maria. Isn't it beautiful?" I dropped a hundred feet until I hovered about 20 feet above the ocean. "This is Johnny's house. Isn't it incredible? You guys, his family is so rich, but they are the sweetest people you could ever hope to meet. Alright, I'm going to fly out over the ocean and see what I can see."

I dropped even closer to the waves, until I was only about 8 feet above the water. I turned over laying on my back as I flew, talking into the camera, occasionally turning back over and reaching down to skim my hands on top of the cool water. "The water is a little cold," I explained. "Oh my goodness! Remind me to tell you guys about my experience falling off the boat."

I flew out further, occasionally rising quickly as I approached a couple of night fishing boats and descending when I felt I was comfortably out of sight. I had just returned to my cruising altitude of 10 feet when I felt a spray of water shoot up from the ocean. I looked down to see a black silhouette emerge from the silver water's surface. A noise that sounded almost like a violin that was out of tune and underwater cut through the calm night air. I flew down closer to the surface as the large whale's massive tail rose out of the water, then slowly slipped underneath again. Behind me I felt another spray of water, as a second whale emerged, this one more massive than the other. Dare I fly closer? Johnny had told me they were gentle creatures when we had seen one out on the boat a few days ago. Always the little dare devil, I flew down, catching the whale's eye. She turned and looked at me for a moment, almost seeming as startled to see me, as I was to see her. I gasped trying to catch my breath as we stared at each other, making sure my phone camera was on her. "Are you guys seeing this?" I whispered, trying not to breathe too hard. "Isn't she beautiful?" She sang her violin song to me, then slowly turned sideways to descend back into the water. Her tail rose out of the water and I flew closer to it. I reached out to touch it as it bobbed out of the water, it's cold, rubbery skin sliding down my hand, tapering off into a scaley end. It slipped silently into the water without even the smallest splash.

I rose higher above the water, looking into the camera and shook my head slowly. "Is this really my life?" I smiled at myself. "Claire, you have to be the luckiest girl in the world."

A shadow fell over as I looked up. The moon slipped behind a massive dark cloud. I looked to the west of the Gulf and saw tiny flashes of lightning popping against the night. This little stinker of a storm had snuck in fast. The whale again rose from the water, calling to me almost as if to warn of the incoming gale.

I smiled down at her. "I'm out of here. Thanks girlfriend."

I flew as fast as I could and within five minutes was back at the bedroom window. I slowly opened it, squeezing in and landing softly on the floor, as raindrops began to pellet the window. The clock now read 2:45 am. In just 5 hours, I would have to get up to catch my 11:30 flight from Tampa to Nashville. I couldn't believe I had been gone for over an hour. I quickly changed into dry, warm jammies and curled up in bed, as the storm blew hard against the window. I had just started to drift off to sleep when I heard my door open. Johnny, unaware that I was partially awake, came in and slipped into bed with me. I felt him slide close up behind me and wrap me in his arms. I melted into them and fell into the best sleep I had in months.

EIGHT

"I CAN'T BELIEVE mom let you drive to Nashville by yourself," I said to Kass as we headed out of the Nashville International Airport the next day.

"Why not?" she asked laughing. "Are you trying to say I'm a bad driver?"

I looked in the mirror at the line of cars behind us. She had been driving 10 miles under the speed limit since we left the airport. Angry drivers flew around us, giving the evil stare, and some were even a little more generous, flipping us the middle finger.

I cleared my throat. "Umm, no. Not at all."

"Kyle and I come to Nashville all the time and he lets me drive, so I'm a pro at this now. Besides, mom had to go into work for a last minute call off."

Mom had recently started a new job at Ft. Campbell

processing the troops in and out of the base, thanks in part to Major Silva's help. I was so grateful for that too. It meant better pay and insurance for my mom and Kass, plus I got to take lunch breaks with her sometimes since she was just down the road. Major Silva had been very kind to my family.

"Major Silva dropped off some of your belongings last night," Kass said, coyly glancing at me sideways.

I looked over at her curiously. She seemed like she was trying to tell me something more.

"Why are you looking at me like that?" I laughed.

"I don't know…" she sighed. "I don't…it's nothing."

"Come on, Kass…" I coaxed her. "That's not fair. You know you can't leave me hanging like that."

"This is going to sound weird though," she said with a little smirk.

"I don't care. I've told you some pretty weird stuff," I laughed.

Kass took a deep breath. "Ok…so Major Silva…" she stopped, shaking her head.

I turned my body towards her and folded my arms looking at her as impatiently as I possibly could. "Kass… tell me."

"Fine. I think Major Silva has a crush on mom," she blurted out as fast as she could.

I stared at her in disbelief. Where did she get that from? She had to be mistaken. "What? Where did you…? What makes you think that?!"

"Because Claire, he seems like he's always trying to

find a reason to come around…and…and mom said that he came over to her work one day to take her to lunch. She said it was to talk about you, but seriously, does he think we're that stupid? Alicia and I both agree he's definitely crushing on mom."

I sat there silent for a moment, scanning my memories for anything that Major Silva had said or done that would make me believe that. I mean, he did brag on her all the time.

"How old is mom?" I asked at last.

"45…and he's 44," she answered before I could even ask.

"Well, how many times has he stopped by since I've been gone?"

"At least three times a week," she said, peering over her John Lennon shades.

"What could he possibly need to stop by that often?" I asked wide-eyed.

"It's always something to do with you, or to help mom with house stuff. Once it was because her brakes were squeaking," Kass said, rolling her eyes. "I mentioned it to mom, but she seems oblivious to it all. She just says he's a nice man."

I sat quietly trying to process what Kass was telling me. Mom was a very beautiful lady, so I wasn't surprised by Major Silva's interest in her, plus she was pretty much the sweetest person to ever walk the planet.

"Now that I think about it, Major Silva does compliment mom a lot to me," I said, almost to myself.

"Well, this can't happen," Kass said defiantly. "Mom doesn't like him... and besides that, she doesn't even know how to date."

I looked at Kass. This time I was the one rolling my eyes. "Seriously Kass, mom is a beautiful woman and Major Silva is actually a handsome man. How do you know she's not interested?"

"Because, she's our *mother*. It's just too weird."

I laughed, "Well, she's also a normal person, with normal feelings, and if she does want to date someone, be it Major Silva or anyone else, it's not our business to tell her she can't."

Kass sighed at my logic. She knew I was right, although deep inside I had to agree with her, somewhat. I couldn't imagine mom dating anyone, much less Major Silva, but I was the older sister, so I tried to keep my head on straight. I did my best to be a good example for Kass and not make a big deal out of things, even when I felt secretly lost myself, and in this situation I was definitely feeling a little lost.

That night Kass, Alicia, and I set up my laptop on my bed and watched all my footage from Florida. I loved watching their faces as I flew them over the ocean. Kass was especially excited about the whale sighting.

"You're right Claire, you have to be the luckiest girl in the world," she sighed repeating the last thing I had said that night over the ocean before I shut the camera off.

"I definitely feel like it," I smiled.

"Let me see that ring again," Alicia said, grabbing my hand. "Oh Claire, it's so beautiful."

My thoughts went immediately to the conversation Johnny and I had the night he gave me the ring, about Alicia and Shawn getting engaged. I so badly wanted to say something, but I had promised Johnny I wouldn't. Alicia already had some idea that he was going to ask her, but she didn't know how or when.

"So what did he say when he gave it to you?" She smiled brightly at me.

"Well, he said that he knows with everything going on right now, that marriage isn't something we can be serious about, but he wanted me to have this to show he is committed to me."

"Awwww!" they cried at the same time.

"That's so sweet Clairey," Alicia said.

"Yeah, it's enough for me right now," I shrugged. "Everything is just so crazy with my job, and the research. This is the only reason why I wish I was normal again. Just because I want everything to be easier for Johnny."

"Well, he loves you just the way you are and that's all that matters," Kass said holding my hand.

"And...he's very lucky to have you," Alicia said, grabbing my other one.

I looked at my baby sister and Alicia (a.k.a. Mony, a nickname I had given her in junior high) and smiled at them both. They were the first to find out that I could fly, Kass on accident, and Alicia on purpose. We had managed to keep it a secret from Lexi. Sometimes I wish that I could have told her, but Major Silva and the higher ups had warned me, no more.

"Thanks you guys," I said. "What about you, Mony? Any more hints from Shawn about the 'M' word?"

Alicia laughed, shrugging her shoulders. "I don't know. I'm pretty sure the question is coming, I just don't know when."

Kass and I gasped in excitement. Alicia and Shawn met the same night Johnny and I did, and they had spent almost every possible moment together since.

Alicia's Hispanic family, especially her mom, had grown to love Shawn after a rocky start and Shawn's African American family loved Alicia like their own. She had spent Christmas break in New York, meeting them at Shawn's persistence, which is one of the things that led us to believe a proposal was not far away.

Kass grabbed Alicia's hand. "So when he does finally get around to it, we are going to plan your wedding BIG, girl!"

"Woah, woah, woah!" Alicia laughed. "I'll definitely be on a limited budget. My parents are doing all they can to help me through nursing school already."

"Not a problem, Mony" I reassured her. "We can make a lot of stuff and hit that discounted bridal store in Nashville!"

"You guys!" she laughed, "I'm not even sure he's going to ask!"

"He'll ask," Kass reassured her.

"Oh yeah, he'll ask," I thought to myself.

NINE

I WENT BACK to work Monday morning, eager to get back into my normal routine. I never grew tired of putting on my Air Force uniform and driving through the gates of Ft. Campbell. I considered myself so blessed to be able to stay in my hometown of Clarksville, Tennessee, so I could be close to my mom and Kass. Part of my agreement to joining the Air Force and letting them guinea pig me and my superpower, was to allow me to stay at the small airfield at Campbell, close to home. So far they had been more than accommodating.

This bright and sunny morning, I had to be at the General's office at 8 a.m. sharp to review the results of my quarterly in Houston.

I sat outside his office door with Major Silva, waiting to be summoned. We waited in silence for a moment, me, curious to see if he would bring up mom, but instead he asked me endlessly about Florida and what had happened when I blacked out. In fact, as soon as this meeting was done I had to go to Blanchfield, (the base hospital) to see Dr. Enroe, who knew very limited information on me.

Major Silva or Johnny usually accompanied me to any doctor's visit, and when we left it was always with a yellow manila folder stamped with the word "Classified." (I once asked Major Silva why they stamped classified on the envelope if they wanted its contents to be secret. I know for me, it would just make me more curious as to what was inside. He laughed and told me it was procedure, but that I had a good point.)

General Collin's secretary looked up in our direction. "Major Silva, Airman Haley, the General will see you now."

I took a deep breath as we stood up. No matter how many times I had been here, and despite his kindness to me, going to see the General was truly intimidating. He was the kind of man that demanded respect without needing to ask for it, but at the same time balanced it all with charisma and a down to earth persona. A perfect example of leadership.

We walked in perfect formation into his pristine office, standing at attention until he released us with an "at ease." His large cherry oak wood desk sparkled under the sleek modern lights hanging from the ceiling, while perfectly aligned certificates and awards too numerous to count, filled the south wall. His office always smelled of a lemon wood cleaner and his spicy scented, old school cologne.

"Have a seat," he said, nodding to the large back leather chairs that sat across from his desk. Major Silva and I sat down, as he picked up a thick folder with my name on it. "Well Haley, I looked over your records from the quarterly and it looks like not much has changed. Are you feeling ok?"

"Yes Sir," I said, not wanting to bring up Florida. I was terrified they would restrict me from traveling and any chance that I might have to go back to Anna Maria again. "I've been feeling great. Nothing's new."

Major Silva gave me an irritated sideways glance, then turned his attention back to General Collins. "Well Sir, Haley did have an incident in Florida I think is important to discuss. In fact, Dr. York thought it was important enough that we bring it to your attention, as well as the higher ups."

General Collins looked at me. "Well Haley, let's hear it," he said, folding his arms and sitting back in his chair.

I took a deep breath and explained the boat incident in as much detail as I could, without trying to over dramatize it.

"Have you ever been unconscious before?" he asked. "I mean, since you've had your flying power?"

"Once, during a high school basketball game…but that was just for a few seconds."

General Collins leaned forward placing both of his arms on his desk, looking me directly in the eyes. "Have you ever lost control of your flying power like this, to where you were flying without any control?"

I fidgeted in my seat. He seemed a bit over concerned. "Well, just when I first started flying. I had to learn to control it with my mind."

"She has no issues when she's sleeping either," Major Silva chimed in.

The General thought for a moment before speaking again. "This concerns me, Haley. My fear is that you'll be out somewhere and black out and the next thing we know, you're off the ground."

I didn't say anything, just nodding quietly. I've learned, sometimes it's better to keep your mouth closed, especially during tricky moments like this.

"How high above the ocean did she float?" he asked looking at Major Silva.

"Angel said about 25 feet," he replied.

The General sat back in his chair again, twiddling his fingers in deep thought. "Alright Silva," he said at last, "I want someone with Haley at all times, at least until we can clear this up. At home, I'm not as concerned, but in training and working, I don't want to risk her hitting her head and passing out. I mean, other than that, I don't know what else we can do."

"Yes Sir," Major Silva said. "Dr. York requested that we go to Blanchfield after this to see Dr. Enroe for a few tests, so I'll let you know what is going on when we get the results from that."

"Alright," General Collins agreed, then turned his

attention to me. "Haley, you do understand my orders, correct?"

"Yes Sir," I said. "But do I have to be chaperoned, even at lunch? Sometimes I get to have lunch with my mom and that seems pretty harmless."

"All the time," he repeated himself. "As long as you're on base and in that uniform, you need to at least have eyes on you. Are you still living off base?"

"Yes Sir."

"Ok, I think it would be in your best interest to move into the barracks."

My face fell immediately. I felt like someone had punched me in the gut. General Collins must have seen the disappointment in my eyes because he quickly added, "It's just a temporary solution, Claire. Remember, this is for your safety and the safety of your family. I really think it would be the best for right now."

"Yes Sir," I said, trying not to sound too disappointed. I knew he was right, but in no way was I ready to leave my mom and Kass. Kass would be graduating next year and I wanted to spend her senior year at home with her. Next year, she was planning on joining her boyfriend Kyle and Lexi, at the University of Tennessee. Kyle played football there and Kass, Alicia, and I were going to be hitting up as many games as we could in the fall.

Major Silva and I left the General's quarters in silence. I could tell he felt bad.

He knew how important my family was to me.

"Claire, I'm sorry. I know how important it is for you

to be with your family. I wouldn't have mentioned the boat accident, but it's my job to pass on vital information and that was pretty vital."

"Thanks Major Silva. I know it's your job, and you guys are just trying to protect me, but I only have this year with Kass before she leaves."

Major Silva paused in the parking lot. "Claire, you remember our talk in Houston, right?" I stopped and looked up at him squinting my eyes in the bright spring sun. "Right?" he asked again.

"Yes, sir," I said while kidnapping and foreign spy images flashed across my mind. It all seemed so far fetched.

"Well, that is a very real scenario that we have to keep in mind, and my job is to make sure you are protected through all of this."

"Ok," I said, disappointed. "I'll pack my stuff this week and be in by the weekend."

That night mom, Kass, and I sat together at dinner discussing Kass and college, my vacation in Florida, and what had happened in Houston. I sat quietly as Kass talked excitedly about Kyle's football scholarship to Tennessee, attempting to pay attention as I tried to think of a way to casually bring up my new housing orders. But who was I kidding? There was no way to casually bring it up, so I waited until Kass was pretty much done with the subject of Kyle.

"So speaking of football and college, I guess I will be moving into the barracks for a while," I said, looking down at my fork, playing with my taco salad.

"Excuse me?" mom said, turning her attention from Kass, who was looking at me, her mouth open in shock.

I cleared my throat. "Yeah, I guess I have to stay there for a while."

"What?! Why?!" Kass asked, her eyes wide.

"It's just temporary..." I started to explain, but Kass cut me off.

"It's because of the blacking out thing, right?"

"I think so...at least part of it."

They both sat quietly for a moment, staring at me.

"Did Major Silva give you these orders?" mom asked softly.

"No, General Collins. He's worried about me passing out, or getting knocked out and floating away." I smirked and rolled my eyes.

"For goodness sake, is that a normal occurrence in your job, Claire?" mom asked. "Getting knocked out?"

"Well, not necessarily," I answered. "A lot of jobs are potentially dangerous, mom...but they do a great job of making sure I'm safe."

I tried my best to constantly reassure her, but my mom was so worried about me all the time. She honestly had nothing to worry about. Major Silva made sure I was protected in bubble wrap most of the time, which I understood, but absolutely hated. I wanted to be treated like the rest of my fellow airmen, and while Major Silva did his best to help me blend in, I still stuck out like a sore thumb. (That's not to say I don't work my little bum off at my job, because I do, but still, having a superpower somehow manages to shine through. I'm not sure that even makes sense, but that's the best way I can describe it.)

Kass was irritated. "Great. So basically, you're not going to be living here my senior year?"

"Kass, I'm sorry. I can't help it. I have to follow orders."

Mom grabbed Kass' hand. "Kass, Claire can't help her situation."

"Kass, you know I would stay home if I could," I reasoned. "I don't want to move, but I have no choice."

Kass looked down at the table, obviously upset. "I know," she mumbled.

I took her other hand. "I'm going to be home as much as I can. I promise. We will hang out just like always, and you can get on base whenever you want with mom's pass. Heck, you can even come to spend the night with me. It will be ok."

That seemed to make her somewhat better, and mom winked her approval at me.

TEN

FRIDAY AFTERNOON, KASS, Alicia, and I unloaded the last few boxes out of my car and carried them into the barracks marked B12, which was right down the road from the busy airfield. I looked out at the traffic control tower remembering the time I had been arrested by Shawn, sneaking into the hangar in search of more of the flying potion.

"I don't know how you're going to live here, Claire," Alicia said as we entered the small single occupant room. "It's so drab and gray. You like everything white and fresh."

"Oh, I'm sure she'll change it up real soon," Kass laughed, setting down my heavy suitcase. They were obviously referring to my OCD. I'm a pretty clean person to a fault. I like everything spotless, fresh, bright, and in order. My room at home reflected that in its various shades of whites and creams.

I sighed heavily, as I plucked my bedding down on the twin bed. Just great. I was used to sleeping in my full. I looked around the room curious as to what I could do to make this place a little more like home.

"Where's Haley's room?" a male voice boomed from down the hall. Alicia peeked her head out into the hallway.

"Down here Shawn," she said, a big smile covering her face.

Shawn appeared in the doorway. "Hi Baby," he smiled, lifting her off the ground in a big bear hug, then looked over at me. "Hey Claire Bear, how does it feel to be sleeping on the airfield legally and not behind bars?"

I squinted my eyes at him, giving him the death stare. "Shut up, Shawn."

Shawn and his friend Devon, who stood behind him, started laughing. Alicia punched him lightly in the arm. "Don't be a jerk."

My thoughts returned to that cold Thanksgiving weekend when I broke into the hangar, desperate to find more of the potion that had given me the power to fly. It had been almost two years, and I could still feel the chill in the air and my body shivering as I flew over the trees that led up to the airfield. I felt a panic knot in my tummy, as I ran from the hangar after being spotted. I had held on tight to the tiny tube of potion that I had miraculously found, then my hopes crushed as Shawn jumped from the trees tackling me to the ground. And his face; horror, panic, disbelief, and disappointment, as I was arrested and escorted from the woods. Johnny had managed to convince Shawn that I was there for a governmental purpose, which is why charges were dropped and I was allowed to go home. Shawn didn't press the issue too much, even with me joining the AirForce. Alicia said he still brings it up from time to time, but she just tells him I told her to drop me off by the airfield that night and that was all she knew. I'm pretty sure he thinks I'm in the Special Forces somehow. Anyway, Shawn just goes with it now. I think he has a lot of questions about me, but he has been very gracious about sweeping it under the rug. I'm hoping someday we can tell him, but for right now the government has been very strict about my superpower. No one is to know and if we leak it, there will be consequences to pay.

I saw Shawn give Kass a little wink and Kass turned to Alicia.

"Hey Alicia, let's go grab that last box," Kass said, taking Alicia's hand and leading her to the door.

"Umm...ok," Alicia said somewhat suspiciously. "Shawn, I'll be right back."

Shawn smiled at her, "Ok, I'll be here." He turned his attention back to me. "Where's your man?"

"He's working until 5. Guard at the hangar, to keep the crazies away," I smirked.

"Oh Claire, you know I'm kidding," he laughed putting one arm around me. I loved Shawn. He treated my best friend so well and Kass and I were crazy about him. Shawn looked over at Devon. "Devon, you got the door?"

"I got it," Devon replied looking down the hall for Alicia.

"So real quick, before Alicia gets back…"

"You're going to ask her to marry you," I said looking up at him.

"What in the…? You and Kass knew!" he laughed.

"We had an idea," I winked at him. "So what's up? You want me to be your best man?"

Shawn laughed, "If Johnny hadn't already claimed that role, it would be a definite yes. Check this out."

Shawn took a black velvet box from his pocket. He opened it to reveal a perfect, rather large round diamond. The outside was surrounded by tiny little pearls, Alicia's favorite. I gasped at the sight of it. "Shawn, she's going to love it! When are you going to ask her?"

"Well, she's coming back with me to visit my family in New York in June. I'm taking her to a Broadway show and then asking her on top of the Empire State Building."

"Aww!" I said, while looking at the ring. "Shawn, that is so sweet and sooo Alicia! She's going to love it!"

"I know," he said, patting himself on the back. "I know what's up with my girl."

I giggled and gave him a big hug. "Thanks for treating her so well. I know you guys are going to be so happy."

"Alright, she just walked in," Devon warned us.

Shawn slipped the box back into his pocket. "Alright

Claire, just tell me and Devon what furniture you need moved."

I began instructing the guys where to move the furniture, trying to open up as much floor space as I could in the tiny room. I sighed heavily as I looked at the limited space. It was half the size of my room at home. Alicia must have noticed my frustration, because she came over and put her arm around me.

"Clairey," she said looking me in the eyes. "This is just a season. It will pass."

I smiled at my forever friend. I was so thankful to have her in my life and I sure was going to miss her when she left. Shawn was a lucky guy.

Later that night Johnny laid beside me on my small twin bed. "These beds are the worst," I laughed pushing down a spring that was stuck in my side.

"You know what I'm going to get you?" he asked, leaning up on one elbow. "A down mattress liner. It made all the difference on my mattress."

"Oh really?" I said turning over and facing him. "You are so sweet to me."

Johnny kissed the tip of my nose. "Anything to make this adjustment easier for you. I know this is not what you want, but selfishly I'm so excited to have you only three blocks away."

"Well, that's definitely a pro in all of this," I said

kissing his cheek softly. Johnny gently tilted my chin up and slid his lips to mine. His arm wrapped around my waist and pulled me closer to him. I had to catch my breath everytime I was this close to him and I broke out into my usual blotchy hives.

"Here comes the blotchies," he smiled.

I blushed, making my blotches even more noticable. I'm sure dating me was not an easy feat for Johnny, and I'm not just talking about the whole superpower thing. Johnny was a completely normal guy and to an extent, I was a totally normal girl with all the feels that comes with dating and being so close to someone. I was so attracted to him. It was hard to just kiss him and leave it at that, but I had decided a long time ago that I was not going to rush into a physical relationship with anyone. I had made a pact with God when I was in middle school and had kept it all these years. Johnny and I talked about it and he was supportive of me in all of it, but I know the struggle was hard for him. It was hard for me too. But here we were. I didn't want to let go of him, and he felt the same for me, so at least I knew it was more than a physical thing between us.

"So have you seen the ring yet?" I asked.

"Oh yeah. About a hundred times," Johnny laughed. "I've never seen Shawn so giddy. That's all he's talking about. You know he wants to get married by October?"

My eyes shot wide open. "October?!" I gasped. "Johnny, that's not going to happen. Alicia needs time to plan a wedding. She can't do that in six months!"

Johnny shrugged his shoulders. "Well, she better get it together because Shawn is on a mission to make it happen."

"Just great," I said, thinking about what a whirlwind our lives were going to become over the next five months. Little did I know what the summer had waiting for me, a drastic turn I could have never imagined, and a mistake that would take me a half a world away.

ELEVEN

ADJUSTING TO LIFE on base was not easy. Even with Johnny three blocks away and other soldiers all around, I felt at times lonely and missed being with mom and Kass every night. I still managed to eat dinner at home a few nights a week and go home for the weekend, plus Johnny and I were double dating with Shawn and Alicia as much as we could.

The weekend before Alicia and Shawn were set to leave for New York, Kass and Kyle, Alicia and Shawn, and Johnny and I had planned a trip to the Cumberland River to swim and picnic on a hot Saturday afternoon. It was the second weekend in June, and Alicia and Shawn were leaving that Monday to go to New York. The girls and I were in our kitchen packing a picnic basket full of our southern favorites: fried chicken, my mom's famous potato salad, baked beans, and sweet tea. The Beach Boys "Fun, Fun, Fun," blared from our speaker and we sang it as loud as we could.

At 10 a.m. Johnny called. "Claire," he said, sounding disappointed.

I motioned for Alicia to turn down the music. "Johnny, are you ok?"

"Claire, Shawn and I can't go today. We've been given a special assignment detail, last minute. We have to report at 1300."

"Oh," I sighed, trying not to sound too disappointed. "It's ok, Johnny. You can't help it."

"I'm so sorry, sweetie. I was looking forward to being with you all day."

Alicia and Kass squeezed in close to me, trying to listen to our conversation.

"What?!" Kass whispered.

"The boys can't come," I mouthed quietly while Johnny continued to talk about how he would make it up to me.

I reassured Johnny it was fine and hung up. Kass and Alicia leaned on the kitchen counter, sulking.

"Great," sighed Kass. "Now, I know Kyle won't go either."

I put my hands on my hips and blew a curly strand out of my face, thinking of what to do. "Well…," I shrugged my shoulders. "How about we go anyway?"

"Seriously?" Alicia asked. "All alone?"

"Why not?" I said, "There's a great spot out by my

grandma's with a..."

"The one with the bridge and the tire swing!" Kass finished for me.

"Yes, that's the one," I laughed.

"Alright, let's go!" Alicia said.

Two hours later, I drove my dark gray Honda down a barely paved road, through thick trees and out into a clearing that gradually led down to a deep creek that branched from the river. Not many people were aware of this little swimming hole back in the woods. An old tire swing hung from a yellow rope attached to an ancient oak tree, whose branches extended far out over the swimming hole. Wild flowers in various shades aligned the banks of the creek, while birds and creatures of every kind flew overhead and scurried down below. Not too far away, we could see the tall bridge that broke from the trees and crossed high above the water's surface. Every now and then, you could hear the old rustic beams moan, as a car or tractor cruised across.

Kass spread the picnic blanket out on a picture perfect patch of grass, as I unfolded a couple of lawn chairs.

Alicia immediately started stripping down to her swimsuit. "Last one in, buys ice cream on the way home!"

Kass and I looked at each other and began a mad dash to get our shorts off and into the water.

We spent the next hour and a half swinging into the

crystal clear water, taking time out to lay in the warm sun, picking out images in the big white clouds that passed over the bright royal sky.

"I'm starving," Kass said at last, sitting up on the blanket and opening the picnic basket.

"Me too," I smiled at her sliding my shorts over my bikini bottoms. "So Mony, are you packed for New York?"

"Yep, I finished everything last night," she said plopping potato salad on her plate.

Kass and I side glanced at each other, soaking in the secrecy of her coming engagement.

I grabbed an apple from the basket. "So what are you guys going to do there?"

"Well, he's being pretty secretive and weird about everything, but we're definitely going to Times Square." She took a bite of her potato salad and then looked at us. "Just between us, I'm pretty sure he's going to propose."

Kass' eyebrows shot up, and I coughed nervously, scared that I would give away the secret. Like I said before, I'm an open book and of all the people in my life, Alicia can read me best.

"What...what makes you say that, Mony?" I asked.

"A-ha!" Alicia said kneeling up on the blanket and putting her face close to mine. "Come on, Claire! Give it up."

Kass leaned in close to me also. "No, you don't Claire. Zip it."

"Kass, you stay out of this," Alicia laughed, pushing

her back on the blanket.

I covered my ears with my hands and started singing "Fly Me to the Moon" at the top of my lungs.

Alicia grabbed my shoulders and started shaking me. I immediately shot 20 feet into the air, still sitting Indian style and singing. I looked down at Alicia and Kass who were looking up at me smiling.

"Claire, get down here!" Alicia laughed.

Kass looked around nervously. "Claire! What if someone's around?"

My eyes scanned the area, confident there was no one. We were pretty secluded out here, plus as always, I had already checked when we first got here. "There's no one!" I yelled down, then continued my song.

"You guys know something!" I heard Alicia yell, throwing a chicken leg up at me. I forgot what a great arm she had, as the chicken leg whizzed past my head, almost hitting my eye.

"Mony!" I yelled down, laughing. "You almost got my eye."

"Good!" she yelled back and then tackled Kass on the blanket below.

"Come on, Kass! Tell me now!" she said, straddling and tickling her.

"Claire!" Kass screamed, giggling hard. "Get her off me!"

I leaned over my crossed legs, looking down at them. "I guess I should help a sister out," I laughed. I was just about to drop on Alicia's back, when the sound of squealing tires cut through the summer air. The bone chilling sound of metal scraping and then a loud boom, snapped our attention towards the bridge. Kass and Alicia jumped from the blanket, as I dropped from the sky. We ran towards the clearing in the trees that gave us a direct view of the bridge.

"Oh God have mercy," Kass gasped. We looked up at a little blue sports car that was dangling over the side of the bridge, tires spinning, and smoke starting to billow from underneath the hood.

Alicia turned and looked at me, her eyes full of terror. "Claire, someone's in there."

I swallowed hard, trying to think of what to do and what I could get away with, as far as flying goes. Flashes of the General's face and CMS Bryant's warnings to me about flying crossed my mind in an instant. No matter, I decided quickly.

What else could I do? The vehicle teetered on the bridge, ready to slide over the edge at any minute.

I turned to Alicia and Kass. "Grab all of our stuff. Don't leave anything. Drive up to the bridge as quick as you can."

They nodded in fear and immediately ran towards our belongings. I pulled my hair back in a messy bun and looked quickly up and down the river, checking to see if anyone was around. It was clear. Standing on a large rock, I looked down at my Saturn rings that began to glow a vivid pink. I hadn't flown since Florida and my body was more than ready.

I flew up and through the trees to lessen my chances of being seen, perching on the highest branch and checked the area once more. No one was in sight. I jumped off the branch and flew down to the bridge, leaning over the rail to see what I was up against. The car had one passenger and rested about 5 feet down from the road. A golden blonde haired girl who appeared to be a little younger than me, was slumped over from the driver's side of the seat and into the passenger's side, her seat belt still in place.

"Hey!" I yelled down, trying to wake her up. "Miss! Wake up!"

The girl didn't budge. I could see, through the driver's open window, that she had a large cut on her arm, that was bleeding profusely. A loud popping sound came from underneath the hood as more smoke billowed out and I knew I had to act fast.

Climbing over the rail, I glided down, softly hovering by the vehicle. The only thing that had stopped its plunge was a large beam that protruded from underneath. The driver's door was jammed against the side of the bridge, and the car lay almost sideways, with the passenger's side facing down towards the river below. The only way to get her out was to go under the car and through the passenger side door. I flew quickly around and opened it gently.

"Omgoodness Claire, be careful!" I looked up to see the terrified faces of Alicia and Kass looking down at me.

I nodded slowly, taking a deep breath and slid into the car. If it gave way, myself and this poor girl would go plunging into the river below. The smoke from the engine blew back into my face as I carefully unlocked the seat belt. To my relief, it slid out effortlessly. I placed my arms around her waist and gently pulled her body toward me. She was a little smaller than me, but still a dead weight. I had never flown with a person my size and hoped my flying powers would hold up under both our weight.

"Oh God, please help her!" I heard Alicia say in desperation.

I tugged again and heard the girl moan. "It's ok," I said to her. "I'm gonna get you out of here." My arms shook nervously and I tried to catch my breath as I pulled her over to me. My heart pounded as the car tipped to the right under our weight and I heard Alicia and Kass gasp in unison above me. I knew I had one shot at flying her out. One more move and this car was gone. I carefully cradled her in my arms, then turned to look behind me at my escape route. I had just a small opening to fly out of. I took a deep breath and pushed against the seat with my legs, bolting us out into the open air as the car rocked hard to the right, then plunged down to the river. I hovered in the air in stunned silence, watching the car crash thunderously into the water below.

"Claire, get over here!" Alicia yelled, reaching an arm out to help me.

I squeezed the girl tighter, then flew up and over the rail where Alicia and Kass stood, eyes wide and hands over their mouths. I landed gently and laid the girl down on the side of the road in a patch of grass. Kass jumped into my arms and Alicia wrapped us both in a bear hug.

"Claire, are you ok?" Kass said, her voice trembling.

"I'm ok Kass," I replied, catching my breath. "Let's check on her."

Alicia knelt down and began checking the girls vitals. "She's breathing normally and has a pulse," she said looking up at us. "Kass, call 911."

Kass ran to the car to get her phone, while I knelt down by Alicia. "We can't stay here and wait for help Mony. Too many questions."

Alicia nodded in agreement with me. "The next car that passes by, we'll go."

As if on cue, an old truck roared around the corner, slowly coming to a stop. "You girls, ok?" A lady asked, rolling down her window.

Alicia stood up to speak to the lady, while I slithered to the car not wanting to be seen. "Ma'am, this girl drove off the bridge. She was able to escape and she seems ok, but her car is in the river. We have help enroute, but I need to get my friend to the hospital. She's hurt too."

"Of course," she said, then pulled her truck to the side.

I jumped into the back seat, as sirens in the distance cut through the air. Kass turned around from the front seat. "Are you ok?" she asked.

"Yeah, we just gotta get out of here before the police come," I said, shrinking down in the backseat.

Kass leaned out of the window. "Alicia! We've gotta go!"

Alicia thanked the woman again and ran over to us, jumping in the car. We sped off toward the main highway, passing a Montgomery County Officer enroute to the accident.

I sat back in my seat looking down at my tattoo that was glowing, and at my hands that were shaking.

"Claire, are you ok?" Alicia asked, looking at me in the mirror.

"Yeah, I'm fine," I answered, pulling my legs close to me and burying my head in my arms. "I just need a minute."

TWELVE

THAT NIGHT KASS, Alicia, and I sat at the dining room table with mom, giving her every detail of the day. Mom sat quietly, but I could see her worry wrinkles popping out.

"Do you think I made the right decision mom? Should I have helped her?"

Mom softly brushed a curl out of my face. "Well honey, think about how terrible you would feel if you hadn't helped. You did the right thing and the only thing you could do, for that matter."

I felt my tummy sink, just thinking about that scenario. She was right. I would never have forgiven myself if that girl didn't survive.

Alicia took my hand across the table. "It's ok, Claire. If you do the right thing, it always works out in the end, even if it's in a way you don't expect."

I smiled back at my sweet friend.

Mom smiled, but was still worried. "So are you certain no one was around?" she asked one last time.

"I didn't see anyone," Kass shrugged.

"I think it's fine mom," I reassured her. "I flew in the trees to the bridge, and then before I flew into open air, I double checked to make sure no one was around."

Mom nodded her head okay, though I could see she wasn't fully convinced. I could relate to that, because honestly, neither was I.

That week at work, I threw myself into my job trying to forget about the craziness of the weekend. Despite how busy I'd been, I couldn't stop thinking about that girl and wondering if she was ok. Each day I had Kass check mom's newspaper and I looked at "Clarksville Now" online to see if anyone had reported the accident.

I don't know if this was the right decision, but I decided not to tell my higher ups about what happened, and I had just casually mentioned it to Johnny. If they didn't need to know, I didn't see the point in bringing it up at all, right?

On Friday afternoon, I jumped into my car and headed home for the weekend. I was so excited to get to sleep in my own bed. Tonight Kass and I were going to cook tacos and do a Netflix binge, and then tomorrow I was spending the whole day in Nashville with Johnny. I couldn't wait. Despite living only three blocks from each other, we worked opposite shifts and the only time I had been able to squeeze in with him during the week was dinner occasionally and if he got the chance to stop by to watch a show on his break at work.

I was just a few miles from home when my phone rang. It was Alicia. I pulled over to a restaurant parking lot to talk to her.

"Hello?"

"Claire?"

"Mony! Omgoodness! I'm missing you girl!"

"I'm missing you too! Did you get the text I sent?"

"Nooo…" I said, putting her on speaker and opening my phone. "Hold on, I'm opening it." I looked down at the pic she sent. The engagement ring Shawn had showed me sparkled on Alicia's perfectly manicured engagement ring finger. In the background the city lights of New York glimmered against a bright sunset. It took a moment for it to register in my mind. Alicia and Shawn were engaged!

"Omgoodness Mony!" I finally said catching my breath. "You're engaged. You're engaged!" I screamed.

"I know!" she screamed back at me. "He just asked me! Of course, you're the first person I had to call! You knew didn't you? I knew it! You and Kass both knew!"

I heard Shawn laughing in the background. "Thanks for keeping your mouth shut, Claire!" He said.

"Tell him 'you're welcome'," I laughed. "Mony, I'm

so happy for you guys!"

"Thanks, Claire Bear. I'm over the moon," she sighed. "When I get back we've got to start wedding planning, ok?"

"Ok!" I exclaimed. "I love you! I'll see you Sunday!"

Ten minutes later I almost ran up the stairs to my house. I couldn't wait to see mom and Kass and spend the evening with them.

"Knock, knock," I said, bouncing in the house. Kass peered from around the kitchen door, shooting me a look of worry.

"Hey Claire," her voice cracked.

"What's the matter, Kass? You and Kyle have a fight?" I joked, throwing my keys and purse on the hallway bench, but she remained serious.

"Come in here."

I dropped my duffel on the floor and headed to the kitchen. Mom sat at the table with Kass' laptop open, reading something intently.

"Mom?" I asked, sitting beside her. My eyes followed her stare to the article online. The first thing I saw was a picture of the bridge. A closer look revealed the blue car dangling and beside it in full view was me. I hovered outside the open car door, cradling the girl in my arms. Next to that was another picture of us, flying just over the brim of the bridge rail. The image was crystal clear.

No way to mistake what was happening in this picture. The headline screamed

FLYING SUPERGIRL SAVES TEENAGER FROM A WATERY GRAVE!

Focusing on the article was hard, as I read aloud each part that stood out the most to me. *"Witness states he was fishing downstream when he heard a loud boom. He then approached the bridge from the south and saw what he thought at first was a large bird flying towards the car, hanging from the side of the bridge.*

The witness, who wishes to remain anonymous, then realized what he was seeing was in fact a girl. "I've never seen anything like this. I haven't slept in a week. I was afraid to come forward at first, but I realized I needed to show the authorities the photos I got on my phone."

Police are not commenting on the accident, but did say they are investigating and are asking for help from anyone who has any information on a gray Honda with three teenage girls seen at the accident. This recent flying girl sighting is the latest in a string of sightings, seen around Clarksville in the last two years."

I stared in silence, my mouth slightly open, and tears stinging my eyes. How could I have been so careless? I was sure no one was around when I went up. I had double checked.

Mom put her arm around me. "It's ok, Claire. Everything's going to be ok."

The tears began to pour and my voice shook in panic. "Oh mom, no it's not! Don't you remember? I'm already on barracks arrest for my episode in Florida. They told me to be careful and I didn't listen." I leaned back in my chair, burying my face in my hands, sobbing. "I'm in so much trouble now. This article is already two days old. I'm sure Silva knows by now."

Kass stood up across the table from us, throwing up both hands in exasperation. "Well, what do they expect, Claire? What else could you do?! Let her die?!"

"I don't know Kass, but now I'm going to lose my career, my power to fly, maybe even Johnny."

Mom wrapped her arms around me. "Oh Claire, you're not going to lose Johnny. He loves you unconditionally and as far as the military goes, I will go have a talk with General Collins. I'm sure he'll understand."

I wiped my eyes and looked at her trying to catch my breath from crying. "Mom, this isn't high school. Thanks, but no. I'm an adult, and an airman at that.

I can't have you going there trying to dig me out of trouble."

Mom slightly nodded her head in agreement with me. I knew she knew she couldn't do that and she was just feeling bad for me. We were all silent for a long moment, as I tried to get my crying under control. Mom was the one to finally break the silence.

"All I keep thinking about Claire, is that you did the right thing. That young girl is still alive thanks to you. You are a hero and we should be celebrating that."

I looked up at my mom. I had never been called a hero and I most certainly had never thought of myself as one. Anytime I used my flying power to help someone, I was too busy worrying over who had seen me or if I would be caught.

"Mom's right, Claire," Kass reassured me. "I know I already said this, but you did the right thing."

I dried my eyes again. "Thanks Kass." I was feeling somewhat better, but was so nervous about facing the General and Major Silva. I wasn't nervous as far as being disciplined. They were always so kind and had told me that my flying power was a lot to carry for someone my age. Anyone in my shoes would have trouble adjusting to it. What I struggled with the most was knowing I had let them down.

My phone rang and I looked down, half expecting it to be Alicia. Major Silva's name popped up and I sighed knowing the conversation that was to come. I picked it up and showed mom and Kass.

Mom looked at me wide-eyed. "It's ok, sweetheart. Go ahead and answer."

I slowly slid my finger across the green circle to answer. "Hello?" my voice croaked.

"Claire."

"Hi, Major Silva."

"Are you home?"

"Yes Sir."

"I'm on my way. Don't leave the house for any reason."

"Yes Sir."

He hung up the phone and I looked over at an anxious Kass and Mom.

"He's on his way here," I gulped.

I was in the bathroom blowing my nose, trying to make myself a little presentable while waiting on Major Silva to come. A million thoughts cluttered my mind. Would he bring the General? Would they be angry? Could I continue my weekend visits home? Lots of questions, but deep inside I knew the answer. My life was about to change completely.

My cell phone ringing interrupted those thoughts. I looked down to see Johnny's name flash across the screen.

"Hello?"

"Claire?"

"Johnny. I'm in so much trouble," I whispered, careful to make sure mom and Kass didn't hear me.

"It's going to be ok, baby. I promise. Listen, I'm on my way to your house with Major Silva. Grab your stuff and be ready to go. We're about 5 minutes out."

"Johnny, what's going to happen? Is Major Silva mad?"

"Don't be scared. We're doing all of this to protect you."

"All of what?!"

Johnny sighed. "Claire, trust me."

I was quiet for a moment. "Ok," I relented.

Johnny cleared his throat. "Oh, and Claire, don't let the semi scare you."

THIRTEEN

"CLAIRE, COME HERE!" Kass yelled from the living room.

I joined her at the living room window, both of us watching wide eyed as a black SUV, followed by a sleek silver and black semi pulled to a stop in front of the house. Mom soon joined us in the living room.

"Clarie, I don't want you going anywhere until I can speak to Major Silva," she commanded me. "I know you're an adult, but I'm still your mother."

"Yes Ma'am," I said. Normally, I would have rolled my eyes and teased her about babying me so much, but this time I wanted her to ask questions. She had a right to know what was happening as much as I did.

Johnny knocked on the door, then opened it. His eyes immediately searched for mine and I went straight into his arms.

"Johnny, I'm so sorry," I whispered as he held me close. I wrapped my arms around him tighter, almost knocking his black beret from his head.

"Everything's going to be fine. I promise," he said in my ear, but looked at my mom to reassure her too.

"Where's Sebastian?" Mom asked him.

"He's talking to the driver. Claire, we need your car keys," Johnny said, slowly releasing his arms from my waist. I had never seen him so anxious before.

"Why?" I asked.

Major Silva appeared in the doorway. "Because we have to take your car, Claire. It's mentioned in the article. This is becoming a frenzy and everyone is looking for it and you...even the police."

"Sebastian, what is going on?" Mom asked.

Major Silva walked to the TV and picked up the remote. "Do you have YouTube on this?"

Johnny joined him, taking the remote from his hand. He typed in a station and immediately a young female reporter began reporting the news.

"I'm standing in front of the bridge here in Clarksville, Tennessee, where last weekend a miracle happened. A miracle no one would ever believe, unless someone captured it on camera.

The camera cut to a dark silhouette of a man, who was obviously trying to hide his identity. The reporter continued, "*A witness, who we will call Larry, claims to have seen a young female fly from the trees in an attempt to save the driver of the wrecked vehicle that hung from this bridge after the accident."*

Larry shifted uncomfortably in his chair, then began his account of that day in his thick Tennessee accent. *"Well, I was down the way fishin' at my usual hole, when I heard a loud boom. I walked up stream a bit and that's when I saw the car hanging from the bridge. I immediately got my phone out to call for help, when out of the corner of my eye, I saw something fly from the tree. At first I thought it was just a large bird of some kind, but I'll be darned if it didn't fly right up to that car. That's when I realized it wasn't a bird, it was a girl. I watched as she climbed into the car and pulled the driver out, then I took out my phone and began snappin' away."* At this time, several pictures of me and the girl began flashing across the screen; me hovering with her in my arms by the car, the car falling from the bridge and splashing into the water below as I looked down, another of us almost to the top of the bridge rail, and at last in flight as we cleared the top of the rail. I gasped with my mouth open, my hand on my chest as I tried to catch my breath, taking it all in. Mom came over and put her arm around my waist and we continued to watch. Larry talked on, *"The next thing I knew another car came out of nowhere, and then the girl fled the area with two other girls in a gray car. I was able to get a picture of the back of it, but barely."*

The reporter finished off the report with, *"Larry stated he wished to remain anonymous out of fear of being labeled mentally unstable and also for the safety of his family. Authorities are looking into the situation, as this has been the latest of many sightings of a flying girl in the Clarksville area over the last year and a half. Police are asking for any information the public may have on this accident or the car in question. Reporting live for Wake Up America, I'm Rebecca Allen."*

Wake Up America. That was a national news program. A very popular national news program that aired all over America.

Major Silva shut the TV off and looked at mom and me. "That was yesterday morning's broadcast. Scores of reporters are in Clarksville now. We have to get Claire and her vehicle out of here."

Mom held my waist tighter as if she was saying no, she would not let me go. "Sebastian," she asked, "is this necessary? Can't you ask the General if she can stay home at least for the weekend?"

"Mary, these orders aren't from the General. These orders surpass the General." He paused for a moment. "They are from Washington."

Mom and I stared at the Major dumbfounded. I fumbled over my words. "Wa…Washington? You…you mean…the Pentagon?"

Major Silva nodded quietly at us, then looked at Johnny. "Angel, get Claire into the SUV." He walked closer to my mom and put a hand on her shoulder. "Mary, I will be here at 0800 hours to pick you and Kass up tomorrow. We are all meeting with the General to discuss our next steps. You know that above all, keeping Claire safe is my number one priority and that's exactly what I'm going to do."

Mom nodded her head in agreement while I hugged Kass tightly. "Watch out for mom, ok?" I whispered in her ear.

"Ok," her voice trembled, but she nodded towards Major Silva who was still talking to mom, "but I think he's got that covered."

I smirked at her remembering our conversation about her "mom and Major Silva's crush theory."

I walked over to mom and hugged her. "Everything's going to be ok, mom. I'll see you tomorrow."

Johnny was right behind me with a hug for her, then threw my duffle over his shoulder. He gently put his other arm around my shoulder and led me outside. We walked out into the warm summer night, where two guards standing outside the SUV greeted us. As one opened the door, I was able to catch a final glimpse of my car being loaded into the semi. Johnny scooted me into the back seat of the SUV, slammed the door shut, and in an instant we were gone.

"Where are they taking my car?" I asked Johnny as we sped off towards Ft.

Campbell.

"We have to put it away, Claire. In fact, I would prefer you to not drive it again."

I leaned forward in my seat, frustration seeping into

my every fiber. "Are you serious?"

Johnny shrugged his shoulders. "What? You can just get a new one," he said softly.

A lump rose in my throat. Oh great, I did not want to start crying again. I swallowed hard trying to push the tears away to no avail. "No, I want that car and I...I want to stay home and make tacos and watch Netflix with Kass."

Johnny put his arm around me and pulled me close to him. "Claire Bear, it's going to be ok." He glanced at the driver, hinting to me that we couldn't talk in front of him.

I sat back in my seat again, melting into his arm that was wrapped around me. Johnny slid closer and I leaned my head against his shoulder. He kissed me softly on my forehead and stroked my cheek. I sighed knowing that even though my life was almost always out of control, this guy was going to stick by me and that made everything much easier to deal with.

We rode in silence for a while, my eyes growing heavier as we approached the base. I was almost asleep when I heard the driver ask Johnny, "What's going on over there?"

Johnny looked to where he was pointing. "Oh man," Johnny sighed.

That got my attention as we merged into the left lane to enter Gate 4. Across the street from the entrance, several news stations had set up, their bright cameras slicing beams of light through the night air. I said nothing to

Johnny, but shook my head in bewilderment and looked at him, asking "what's going on?" with my eyes.

Johnny slightly raised his shoulders, giving me the universal "I have no idea" sign.

"The President must be coming to base," the driver guessed.

"I'm not sure," Johnny replied as we continued to watch the chaos. "I haven't heard anything about that. You know the media though, always making a big deal about nothing."

The driver laughed, agreeing with Johnny.

Fifteen minutes later, we pulled through another set of gates surrounding the Ft. Campbell jail. I looked at Johnny in shock as the driver talked to the gate guard, showing him proper ID to pass through.

"The jail?" I whispered incredulously.

"It's the best guarded facility on the base," Johnny replied and then put a finger to his lips, silencing me to secrecy.

My thoughts turned back to my seventeen year old self, being driven through these very gates, handcuffed in the back of a Military Police SUV, scared out of my mind. I had been arrested for trespassing on the airfield in search of more of the secret formula that had given me the power to fly. I had vowed to never return to this jail again, but here I was.

Johnny squeezed my hand as we drove around to the back of the building. The driver paused as we came to a small four way stop. Headlights behind us caught my attention and I noticed another black SUV close on our tail. I looked at Johnny.

"Silva," he whispered.

The road turned into a small driveway that wound through thick trees and brush. At last we pulled up to another gate and guard. Beyond the gate a beautiful brick home stood in the moonlight, surrounded by tall trees.

The SUVs came to a sudden stop in front of the circle driveway. The driver opened the door and Johnny grabbed my bag and another in the back, as I walked toward the front steps of the house. Major Silva soon joined me, pulling his phone out of his pocket and punching in a code to unlock the door.

"I'm staying here?" I asked.

"You think I was going to put you back in the brigade?" he laughed, his thick Spanish accent, the strongest I've ever heard it. "Come on in, Claire."

Johnny and I followed him. The house was beautiful. All wood floors, a tall fireplace, vaulted ceilings, and the whitest kitchen I had ever seen.

"So this is what it looks like," Major Silva said, looking around.

"What is this place?" I asked.

"Well, let's put it like this," he smiled. "The last guest to stay, occupied the White House."

I gasped. "The President?"

Silva nodded his head. "It's the most secure place on Campbell and that's why you're here."

I shrugged my shoulders. "Major Silva, it's just a few

nosey reporters. They're gonna snoop around for a bit and then go back to wherever they came from."

Major Silva shook his head in disbelief. "Claire, didn't you pay attention to anything CMS Bryant told you in Texas? It's not the reporters we're concerned about. It's the sharks the reporters can bring."

I looked at him, recalling my conversation with him and CMS Bryant. Sharks meaning foreign spies. I know that sounds very "James Bond" and sometimes I want to laugh inside thinking about it, but they seemed to think it was a very real possibility.

"I remember," I said.

He looked at Johnny. "Angel, did you cancel your flight training for tomorrow?"

"Yes Sir."

"Alright Haley, Angel will stay here with you tonight. I will send a driver to pick you up in the morning. I want you both in dress blues." He turned and looked at me as he headed towards the door. "Yours are hanging in the bedroom closet," he said reading my mind, before I could ask.

The door closing behind him echoed through the hollowness of the house. Yes, it was beautiful, but it had an unlived feeling to it. Like a body with no soul.

Johnny walked up behind me and wrapped his arms around my waist. "Can you believe this place?"

"It's beautiful," I said, trying to sound cheerful. I turned and looked into his bright green eyes. "You had to cancel flight training tomorrow for this?"

"Well, yeah," he smiled.

I felt terrible. I knew how much he loved flying and I knew first hand how disappointing it was to miss a chance to go up. "That sucks, Johnny. I know how important flying is to you."

Johnny looked down and kissed my forehead. "Yeah, but you're more important, Claire. You're more important to me than flying could ever be. I would give up a thousand flights for any amount of time with you."

I wrapped my arms around him and squeezed tight. Was this guy even real? I didn't know what I'd do without Johnny through all of this. I mean, I knew I had Major Silva and he had been so good to me, but Johnny was holding my hand, walking me through all the uncertainty.

Johnny ran his hand up the back of my neck and into my long curls, careful to stay at the roots and avoid turning my hair into a total frizzy mess. I had taught him well. He leaned down, touching his lips to mine. I went on my tippy toes to return his kiss. Not that I have anyone to compare him to, but I'm pretty sure he is the best and sweetest kisser in the world.

"Have you eaten?" he asked at last.

I shrugged my shoulders, letting him know that I hadn't.

Johnny smiled, "Come'on Claire. Let's see what they got to eat in that pristine white kitchen."

Johnny opened the refrigerator, as I stood close by him, not wanting to let go of his arm. "Hmmm…so what are you in the mood for?" he asked.

I looked at all the veggies and fruit that stocked the shelves, then opened the freezer. A frozen cheese pizza caught my eye.

"How about we chop up some veggies and throw it on that pizza?" I suggested.

"Ok, you little mind reader," he laughed.

Thirty minutes later, Johnny and I sat on the comfy overstuffed couch, the pizza in front of us watching the latest episode of Cobra Kai, my new screen time addiction. The pizza looked so delicious, but my tummy was too nervous thinking about the meeting tomorrow and what was to come.

I played around with the cheese on my pizza. "Johnny, what do you think is going to happen tomorrow?"

Johnny finished chewing a bite and paused for a moment, choosing his words carefully.

"Do you think I'm in trouble?" I asked before he could answer.

"Claire, I honestly have no idea what's going to happen." He took my hand. "But I do know that you're not in trouble. I can tell you that Major Silva and the Air Force have your best interest at heart. I don't think you realize what a miracle you are. You're a national treasure and they want to protect you."

Wow, a national treasure. I felt like I had been more of a pain in the rear, than a national treasure and I'm sure there were a lot of higher ups that agreed with me. I smiled at him, though. That made me feel a little better.

Johnny always knew just what to say. He wrapped his arm around me. "But at the end of the day, you're ultimately my responsibility and I would never let anything happen to you."

I leaned over and kissed him again. I couldn't keep my lips off him. "I feel so safe with you, Mister. I don't know how I could handle all of this without you."

Johnny put his plate to the side and moved closer to me. His eyes were intense, yet guarded. He slid his other arm around me and pulled me closer. My hand had a mind of its own, moving around the back of his neck and pulling his lips to mine again.

I don't know why I felt so much desperation and panic. I had some strange feeling inside of me, almost as if I was going to lose him through all of this. I was afraid this would be my last chance to be alone with him for a while and I only had a little time left to kiss on this sweetness.

Little did I know how true that would be.

FOURTEEN

SIX A.M. CAME early the next morning. Johnny and I had stayed up past midnight, but I woke easily. Anxiety seems to be a great energy source for my body.

I showered and threw on my AC uniform, careful to take extra time on my makeup and hair, even though I had to pull it back anyway. Johnny soon appeared in the bedroom doorway.

"Are you ready to go beautiful?"

I gasped when I saw him. He looked so handsome in his dress blues. "You look amazing," I smiled.

Johnny walked over and pulled me close. "I was just going to say the same for you."

I looked up at him, trying to hide my anxiety, but of course he saw right through me. "Claire, everything's going to be fine," he reminded me for the hundredth time.

The sound of the doorbell chiming interrupted our conversation, the door opened and a Sergeant called up from the foyer, "Angel, you guys ready?"

Johnny looked down and kissed my forehead. "Let's go, sweetie."

The sun burned bright in my tired eyes, that immediately found my mom and Kass standing on the steps of the General's office building. My mom seemed to be deeply engrossed in a conversation with Major Silva. Mom has always been a kind and passive person, but since she found out I could fly, she had become this protective momma bear, asking tons of questions and offering a lot of advice into my well being. Not to sound like a baby, and not that the military officials hadn't been good to me, but it made me feel a little safer knowing she was there.

Kass spotted me and waved, helping to melt some of the tension I felt inside.

My Kass was such a beautiful person inside and out. Today she looked exceptionally so in her baby blue sundress that popped against her long sandy blonde hair and olive skin.

The driver pulled up to the main steps and I immediately jumped out, eager to greet my mom. She had looked so stressed last night when I left and I wanted to make sure she was okay. Mom immediately held her arms out to hug me.

"Hey Mom," I said. "Are you guys ok?"

"Are you ok?" Kass asked. "The media outside of base is insane."

"They're still out there?" Johnny asked joining us.

"Yeah, and worse than last night." said Major Silva, looking around suspiciously, then putting his arms around me, mom, Kass. "Alright ladies, let's get inside."

Major Silva led us through the glass doors and into McAuliffe Hall. Our footsteps echoed through the vast empty foyer, vacated for the weekend. I was half expecting to be ushered to the General's office, but was surprised when we were led to an elevator at the end of a long hallway I had never noticed before. Major Silva pushed an unmarked button that immediately descended three stories to the basement.

The elevator dinged and we were greeted by another long, overly polished hallway. Kass looked at me skeptically and I shrugged my shoulders, biting my lip, letting her know I had no idea where we were going either.

The door at the end of the hallway opened into a modest, but very modern conference room. A long shiny black table with high black office chairs lined each side of the table, sixteen total. The gray walls were lined with sparkling, silver picture frames circling the faces of each of Ft. Campbell's generals and their duration of service.

General Collins and two very decorated men stood on the other side of the table. The drill was so familiar to me, going into conference rooms and meeting very distinguished and intimidating gentlemen, but this meeting somehow felt different. Not as warm and welcoming as previous meetings. These were the higher ups I had heard about only in passing. I followed Major Silva and Johnny's lead, filing in and standing at attention until told otherwise. Mom and Kass waited outside the room as instructed to do, until given permission to enter.

General Collins cleared his throat. "At ease soldiers. Sirs, may I present Major Silva, Warrant Officer Angel, and of course, Airman Haley.

Each of the higher ups reached out to shake our hands, then General Collins pointed toward the door cueing mom and Kass to enter. "Please come in Ms. Haley. Gentlemen, this is Ms. Haley, Airman Haley's mother, and her other daughter Kass. The men shook my mom's hand and smiled cordially, but still the level of uneasiness remained.

General Collins invited us all to sit, our crew on one side and theirs on the other.

A tall African American man, who the General had introduced as Command Sergeant Major Williams spoke first. "Well let me first say Airman Haley, this meeting should have taken place a long time ago. As leaders, we should have already taken the time to come down and meet you, so we apologize for that. On behalf of the United States Military and the leadership we represent, we want to apologize for the situation you are now in. Had we known the flying formula existed, we would have tracked it down and did everything we could have, to protect innocent people, such as yourself, from the effects of it." He paused for a moment and looked at General Collins. "On the flip side of that, who would ever believe anything like this could be possible? It's something we are still trying to wrap our minds around and process, and as you know, doing all we can to make sure you are physically ok." He cleared his throat and nodded at the decorated officer in the Air Force uniform. "Lieutenant General Gray and I have been following your situation and monitoring your progress, myself on behalf of the Army and he, on behalf of the Air Force. We have been allowing you to remain here, because we know your family lives here and your desire to live by them," He paused for a moment and gave me a kind but firm glare. "but I think the time has come for us to revisit your homebase situation."

I deflated inside, unable to hide my disappointment. I pretty much knew this was what I had coming, but hearing it still floored me. How was I going to leave mom and Kass…and my Johnny? Out of the corner of my eye, I saw Johnny exhale a small sigh of disappointment also.

Lt. Gen. Gray looked at me, acknowledging my obvious disappointment. "We have a job to do Haley. We have to protect the United States military, but more importantly, protect you. I understand that you were put in a difficult place and we agree that you did the right thing in saving the girl's life, but in the meantime, your life is now potentially in danger. That newspaper article shows a lot of your face and a description of your vehicle and we just have to do something to keep you out of situations like that."

I heard my mom's voice from behind me. "Excuse me, what do you mean her life is in danger?"

General Collins looked at me. "Claire, have you told your mom anything about what was discussed in Texas?"

I shifted uncomfortably in my chair. "Well...no Sir. I didn't think it was necessary." I turned and looked at mom.

"Well?" she asked, concerned.

I stared at the ground hesitant to give her anything else to worry about.

"May I?" Major Silva asked, noticing my hesitation. I nodded yes to him.

"Mrs. Haley, in Texas it was discussed with Claire, that there is a chance of her life being in danger. What we mean by that has nothing to do with her flying or her health. Our concern is for other countries and predators who are eager to get their hands on someone like Claire for their own selfish gain."

"You mean like spies?" Kass gasped.

Major Silva slowly shook his head. "Pretty much or just crazy people in general. That's why we moved her to the barracks in hopes that we could protect her more. But now with this out and scores of reporters bearing down on us, we need to act quickly."

"Very true," General Collins agreed. "And questions about you Haley, are starting to come to me now, instead of the Clarksville Police Department."

Everyone was quiet for a moment, and mom put her hand on my shoulder. "Claire, why didn't you tell me?"

I sighed heavily. "Mom, I didn't want you to worry. You have enough on your plate."

I could tell mom was irritated with my choice of secrecy. She looked straight ahead, tongue in cheek, her brow furrowed.

Johnny spoke up. "So what does all this mean for Claire?"

CSM Williams picked up a thick manilla envelope and handed it to me. "Airman Haley, we are going to assign you as far away as we can, without sending you out of the country. Now, please understand, this is temporary until we can reevaluate your status. In six months, we will meet together again and see how things stand and we'll go from there."

I nodded my head in agreement, unable to speak. I managed a quiet, "Yes Sir," but what else could I say? I couldn't argue with orders. Dramatic scenes of being locked up in some compound in the middle of nowhere flashed across my mind.

Lt. Gen. Gray pointed at the envelope that laid across my lap. "You're being assigned to Hickam Air Force base in Hawaii, Haley. We are putting you with a special detail unit. We chose Hawaii, because it's off the mainland and we can do better testing on you."

I couldn't believe my ears. Hawaii? I had dreamed of going to Hawaii since I was a little girl. My heart skipped a beat, thankful I wasn't being shipped off to no man's land, but also at the thought of being away from my family and Johnny.

"May I ask what kind of testing?" I asked, curious about the name "special detail" unit.

"Well, pretty much what you've been doing in Houston," Lt. Gen. Gray explained. We will continue with all the progress you have made out there and will still keep in touch with Dr. York, only he will come to you. We don't want you to leave the island for awhile."

I looked back at my mom and was surprised to see some relief in her eyes. She nodded at me. I knew she was sad to know I was going, but her worry about my safety far outweighed her desire to see me on the weekends.

General Collins wrapped up some last minute details. "Alright, so Haley tomorrow night at 23:00 hours you'll be departing. You and your family are welcome to stay at the guest quarters until then, to say your 'see you laters' for now. Angel will escort you to the barracks where you'll have one hour to pack your belongings and be back at the guest quarters. From then on, you are not permitted to leave the quarters until your flight leaves. Is that understood?"

"Yes Sir," I replied.

We all stood and were formally dismissed. I shook hands with and thanked the higher ups. Lt. Gen. Gray whispered in my ear, "You can thank Gen. Collins for your placement at Hickam. He really fought for that."

"Yes Sir," I smiled at him.

FIFTEEN

JOHNNY AND I sat quietly in the back of the SUV on the way to my barracks. I could tell he was not his normal self. When Johnny is upset, he shuts down and becomes quiet. I usually give him his space, but today I felt desperate to talk to him, in that we only had so much time together.

"Johnny…" I said looking at him.

He turned his head from his stare outside the window. I don't know that I had ever seen so much distraught in his eyes. He smiled gently at me.

"I'm so sorry," I whispered. "If I could give it all up to stay here with you, I would."

"It's ok, Claire," he answered, but I knew it wasn't ok. I knew he was hurt, but was trying to hide it to protect me and the time we had left together. Inside I secretly trembled, my insecurities getting the best of me. Maybe this was the thing that would finally drive him to end everything. I know my flying power was a lot to handle.

We arrived at my barracks and packed my room as quickly as we could. Luckily, I didn't have much there anyway. I had this feeling when I moved in I wouldn't be staying long, so I didn't get too comfy.

After Mom and Kass went home and grabbed a few of my belongings they met us back at the guest house with Major Silva. Kass oohed and aahed over every room in the house and luckily I had an extra swimsuit she could borrow for the pool in the back.

We cooked out and had dinner together for what we knew would be our last one for a while. Kass, never one to hide her feelings like me, was clearly depressed, and despite mom's attempt to stay upbeat about everything, I knew she felt the same.

I watched with curiosity as Major Silva, relaxed in his civvies, gave my mom his undivided attention. Who could blame him? My mom was beautiful, kind, wise, and the most perfect being ever. Mom in return, definitely didn't shy away from his attention. I think Silva has made her feel safe through this whole crazy thing, something she hadn't felt since dad died. I'm starting to think Kass was right about this little thing happening between the two of them and I didn't mind at all. I felt better knowing he would be around while I was in Hawaii.

"Let me again reiterate to everyone, that no one is to

know where Claire is," Major Silva reminded us. "As far as we know, she's simply away training."

"Sebastian," I interrupted him. "Alicia? I can't not tell her where I am."

"Claire, these are not my rules," he reminded me. "They are straight from the top."

"But she was there. She's in the article too," I argued. "Someone's going to have to warn her before she gets back tomorrow."

He paused for a moment, realizing I was right. It was not fair to have Alicia walk into everything blind. "Ok," he agreed. "Let me clear it with the General and we'll go from there." He held one finger up in warning, "but until then not one word."

Late that night, after mom and Kass had gone to bed, Johnny and I laid back in one of the lounge chairs by the pool gazing up at the black starry sky. My Saturn ring tatt glowed brightly, beckoning me into the dark heavens. I hadn't flown since the accident and I so badly wanted to rocket out into the night and leave all my earthly stress behind. My flying power was such an awesome gift and I was so tired of hiding it.

"Mr. Tatt is glowing pretty bright there," Johnny laughed.

"I know," I smiled and snuggled closer to him. "I wanna fly so bad, Johnny."

"I know," he replied, kissing my forehead. "Maybe someday you won't have to hide it anymore Claire, but for right now we have to keep you safe."

"I'm so sorry," I apologized for the hundredth time. "I know I make your life difficult."

Johnny leaned back and looked me in the eyes, slightly irritated. "Claire, I want you to stop saying that," he said kindly, but with a sternness. "You know it's not true. You fill my life with excitement and fun…and…and love."

I smiled at him. "You're in love with me, Johnny."

He laughed, rolling his eyes. "I know, Claire. You're in love with me too."

I teased him a little more. "In fact, I'm so sure you're just *so* in love with me, you pretty much couldn't live without me."

"I wouldn't go that far…" he teased.

"Oh no, it's true," I interrupted, my eyes full of mischievousness. "You would just be a boring helicopter combat pilot without me. No action ever."

"Oh, no action, huh?" he said, putting a finger beside the ticklish side of my neck. I squirmed even though he hadn't even touched me yet. "What's the matter with you?" he laughed. "I'm not even touching you."

I grabbed his finger in a lame attempt to keep him from tickling me, but that didn't work at all.

"Nice try Airman Hailey, but you're just a little too wimpy for me."

I gasped at his insult and began the ultimate struggle to gain control of his hands, before I got the tortuous tickle that he was so good at.

"No Johnny." I screamed. Too late. Johnny slid his hand around the back of my neck sending chills down my body, then gave me the worst tickling of my life. I wiggled and squirmed, trying to catch my breath between laughs, but was no match against him.

"What was that you said?" he laughed.

"Nothing!" I lied.

"I believe your exact words were 'boring helicopter combat pilot?' You should probably take that back, Claire."

"NEVER!" I giggled, pulling up my shoulders to avoid more tickles by my neck.

"You are so stubborn!" he laughed, tickling me even harder. "Just give up!"

"Not happening!" I gasped, laughing even harder. I looked at Johnny's sweet smile. I loved being with him so much. All at once the thought of leaving him hit me hard. I had been so busy, too caught up in the drama of the last two days to think about how much it would hurt being away from him. Everything had happened so fast, I just couldn't wrap my mind around it. My eyes began to tear up and my neck turned bright red like it always did when I was emotional. My bottom lip quivered, as I tried hard to keep the tears from surfacing further.

Johnny looked down at me, noticing my weepy eyes. "Claire, are you ok? Did I hurt you?"

That was all it took for the dam to break. I began sobbing uncontrollably. "Johnny...Johnny, I don't want to leave you again," I cried like a baby. I wrapped my arms around him, pulling my body as close to him as I could. "I'm so tired of all this. I just want to be with you."

Johnny pulled me tight to him, his familiar scent enveloping me. "Claire Bear, I don't want you to leave, but everything's going to be ok." He lifted my chin and wiped a tear from my wet cheek. "Listen to me, I'm going to be here for you no matter where you are, and no matter where I am. We'll get through this little separation and then I'm never going to let you go again."

Johnny reached down and kissed me. I bet he's kissed me a thousand times in our two year relationship, but each one is always as special as the first and I never want him to stop. I kissed him over and over again, knowing this time tomorrow night, I would be craving his lips on mine. Johnny didn't seem to mind and he returned my kisses until at last we drifted off into an exhausted sleep.

Sunday I spent the whole day with Johnny and my family. Major Silva was able to get clearance for Alicia to come to the guest house. She showed up an hour before I had to leave for the airfield and all alone, since Shawn was still unaware of my flying power.

After Kass and I oohed and aahed over her beautiful ring, Alicia and I sat alone on the couch and I filled her in with the details of the last two days.

"Hawaii, Claire?" she asked less than thrilled. "How

long do you have to stay there?"

I shrugged my shoulders. "I guess until this all cools down."

"So no time limit?" she sighed annoyed and loud enough so Silva could hear her. "How can they just ship you off with no timeline?"

"It's for my safety, Mony," I reassured her.

Alicia shook her head unconvinced. "Will we be able to contact you? We were going to plan my wedding."

I put my arm around her. "I know. I've been thinking about that and I promise I'm going to help no matter what."

"This sucks," Alicia said, hugging me tightly. " I'm going to miss you Claire, but I'm so glad you'll be safe."

"Thanks, Mony." I lowered my voice. "Please watch out for Kass while I'm gone. I'm so worried about her."

Alicia took my hand. "I got her, Claire...and your mom."

I felt my eyes tear up again. "Her senior year and I'm going to miss it all."

"Maybe this is just for a few weeks, until everything calms down," she tried to reassure me.

I shook my head no and lowered my voice. "I think we both know it's going to be longer than that. I'll be lucky if I'm back by Christmas."

Alicia sat closer to me and put her arm around my shoulder. "Well, I'm praying this will pass quickly and you'll be back before you know it."

I love my sweet friend. I hugged her and kissed her

cheek. "Thanks, Mony."

An hour later I was standing in the office of the hangar at the airfield hugging my family goodbye.

My mom hugged me tightly. "We'll see you again real soon. You'll be safe there for now," she said trying to make me feel better, but more so for herself.

I nodded in agreement and hugged her back. "I love you, mom."

Johnny walked over to me, with my large duffle slung over his shoulder. "You gotta get moving, sweetie."

I hugged mom, Kass, and Alicia one more time. Major Silva smiled at me and I walked over to him. "You're in good hands, Claire," he said. "But if you need anything, know that I'm always here for you. I'll take the first flight to Hawaii, you know that."

"Yes Sir," I half smiled. I hugged him and he half hugged back, looking down at me somewhat surprised. Major Silva seemed to not be much of an affectionate person. Maybe it's because he had too much military in him, or that he had never been married or had a family, but he seemed to soften with my embrace. "Take care of mom," I whispered, winking at him.

He smiled slyly at me, almost embarrassed. "I got them," he said, nodding at Kass and mom.

Johnny's hand slipped into mine and we headed out the door to the tarmac. I turned and looked at my family one last time, waving bye. My mom smiled holding back her tears and Alicia wrapped one arm around Kass to reassure me she was going to be ok.

Johnny and I walked to the small jet that was waiting, its engines roaring, ready for take off.

"They're flying you to San Diego and from there, Hawaii," he said above the noise.

"Thanks," I said, hugging him tightly.

"Claire," Johnny said, leaning into my ear. "I love you. I love you so much and I'll be here waiting for you."

"I love you too, Johnny. So much."

He kissed me once more and I held him tight, not wanting to let go. At last I did and walked to the plane. A tall, dark man who could easily play defensive line for the Tennessee Titans greeted me at the top of the steps. I noticed his side arm and badge, peeking out from under his black dress coat jacket. My thoughts immediately went to Will Smith in *Men in Black*. This man could have been his twin, except for the extra 20 pounds of muscle on him.

"Hello, Airman Haley," his deep voice boomed. "I'm Special Agent In Charge Lucas and I will be escorting you to Hawaii."

"Thank you," I said, shaking his hand and then finding my very roomy seat in the front row, by the window. The entire empty cabin, though small, looked first class.

"Wow. Secret Service," I thought to myself.

Mr. Lucas found a seat across the aisle from mine and stretched out his long legs. I noticed his hot pink and black striped socks that peeked out from underneath his pants legs and smiled to myself.

I looked out of the window, watching as Johnny walked to the hangar. He turned and stood by the door waving, as we pulled away.

I sat back in my seat, trying my best not to lose it in front of Mr. Lucas and swallowed hard to keep myself from crying. I put in my ear phones, in hopes of driving my emotions away. I know this sounds weird, but I hate crying in my uniform. It makes me feel weak.

Mr. Lucas settled in looking like he was ready to nap and who could blame him. It was almost midnight.

The jet's engine roared and I grasped the seat as Journey's *Don't Stop Believing* pumped into my Ibuds. The jet shot down the runway at a super force speed, rocketing into the black starry night. Once we leveled off, I looked over at Mr. Lucas who was dozing already. He seemed to take the take off in stride, making me believe he did a lot of flying.

I leaned back in the cushy seat, my eyes growing heavy, and drifted off into a restless sleep.

SIXTEEN

THE CLOUDS BROKE beneath me as I descended above the rolling waters of an ocean, to a large marina dock in the distance. My eyes adjusted to the setting sun and I gazed hard, trying to make out the tiny specks that covered the dock. Small brilliant flickers of light popped, making the dock look like a glistening diamond. I rubbed my eyes, unsure I was seeing what I actually thought I was seeing. Were those people? They scurried in a frenzy as I flew closer. They were people. A large crowd with cameras flashing and phones faced towards me capturing my every move. I immediately turned toward the sky, searching for a giant cloud I could hide safely behind, but my body had a mind of its own. I tried to push myself into the sky to no avail. I had no control. My body did as it pleased. I looked at my tattoo rings that had faded to a light gray, barely there with *all traces of pink gone.*

I gasped as I came closer to the crowd that looked up, their eyes full of astonishment, unbelief, and horror. A loud roar came up from the crowd. "How can this be?" "Is that a girl?" someone asked. "IT'S AN ALIEN!" someone else yelled.

They slowly parted as I landed in the middle of them all. I couldn't even control where I landed. How did they know? Who told on me? I turned around frantically looking for a way out, as they began to swarm. A strong hand grabbed my arm and spun me around. Johnny looked down into my eyes, his face pale and emotionless. "Claire," he whispered. "I had to. I had to tell them." He shook my shoulder softly. "Claire?"

I woke with a start, Mr. Lucas calmly shaking my shoulder. "Claire?" His deep voice boomed. "We're descending."

I shuddered from the horrible dream I had just woken from, thankful to be safe in the jet. "Ok," I said, wiping my eyes and adjusting to the bright yellow sunset shooting through the cabin windows. "Thank you, Mr. Lucas."

The wheels of the jet touched softly down on the tarmac of Hickam Air Force base. It was 4 pm Hawaii-Aleutian Standard Time. I had been traveling for over 18 hours at this point and was so exhausted. The pilot taxied to the gate at the very south end and came to a stop. I stood up to grab my overhead bag, but Mr. Lucas stopped me with a gentle tug on my arm.

"Hold on a minute."

I watched as he walked down the steps of the plane, looking around first, then greeting the two officers who were there to meet us. He showed his ID and badge, then shook hands. This was so weird. I felt like some kind of secret package that was being delivered.

Mr. Lucas quickly scaled the steps. "It's ok now," he said.

I set down my backpack to shake his hand. "Thank you, Mr. Lucas."

He looked down at my outstretched hand and smiled. "I'm going with you. All the way. Orders from the top," he smiled, pointing up.

"Oh, ok," I smiled back, then followed him out onto the plane stairs. A blast of salty pacific ocean air hit me in the face and enveloped my body. I looked over the vast air field. It was so much bigger than Campbell's. A pang of sadness made my tummy drop, thinking about home. As beautiful as Hawaii was, I didn't want to be here. I wanted to be there, with my family and Johnny.

As if he could read my mind, my text dinged from Johnny. I would text him in a little bit. Right now I had to shake hands with some very important looking men.

We reached the bottom of the stairs and Mr. Lucas spoke up. "Gentlemen, this is Airman Haley."

I dropped my bag and immediately stood at attention, saluting the very high ranking officers. The taller, older man looked me up and down, as I stood as straight as I possibly could. I could only see him out of the corner of my eye, but I could definitely sense his coldness toward me. He turned to his partner (a middle aged Asian man) talking out of the side of his mouth, but I could clearly hear what he had to say.

"This is what all the fuss is about? A girl?"

I watched the other officer shrug his shoulders and heard him sigh loudly. I'm not sure if it was a sigh of frustration and he was agreeing with his friend, or more in irritation about his question.

I glanced at Mr. Lucas without moving my head. He had one eyebrow cocked up, staring at the two men, as if they had insulted him. He walked closer to the officers, lowering his voice and pulling folded paper work from inside his dress jacket. "Sirs, I have been given direct orders from Washington to make sure this young lady arrived here safely. Now, I don't know the details of this assignment or why she was sent here, but I will be accompanying her and making sure she arrives at her final destination...so if you could point us in the right direction I would appreciate it."

Everyone was silent for a moment, then the older officer spoke up. "We're going to Lt. General Gray's office. Mr. Lucas, you can ride in the back with..." he paused and looked at my name tag, having forgotten my name already. "Airman Haley."

Mr. Lucas nodded and grabbed my duffle. "Let's go, Claire."

I took that as my dismissal from the officers and followed Lucas to the black SUV. He opened the door for me and then got in on the other side. "Man, I was at least expecting a lei," he said sarcastically. "You better be worth all this trouble girl," he winked at me.

"Oh, Mr. Lucas," I smiled, a little cocky. "I'm so worth all this trouble."

The drive to the General's office was short, only taking 10 minutes. I was grateful for that, because I don't think it could have gotten any more awkward in that SUV. No one said a word as I looked outside the window, curious to see what my new home for the next however many months was going to look like. So far, Hickam looked like a beautiful place.

We pulled in front of a modest, stone building and then headed toward the door.

"Excuse me Claire," Mr. Lucas said, pushing past me to make sure he entered first. I was very curious as to what the military had told him about me. I could tell he was just as curious about who I was and why it was necessary for him to escort me all the way to Hawaii, but he didn't dare ask and was very much a professional. I wish I could have told him. Sometimes I just want to tell everyone and not have to worry about all the secrecy anymore.

We were escorted into the building. Mr. Lucas paused patiently at the door, while I stopped to examine a small lizard type reptile climbing the wall.

"Oh, look how cute!" I exclaimed. We definitely didn't

have those little critters in Tennessee.

A blast of cold air pushed the humidity out of the doorway and I felt little chill bumps spread across my arms in the sudden change in temperature. We followed a long hallway that led to another long hallway, turning right. A secretary at the last office greeted us and eyed me curiously as the officers announced our arrival. She didn't look much older than me and seemed to know we were coming. I returned her stare with a smile and she snapped out of her glare, smiling quickly when she realized I caught her staring.

"I'll let Lt. General Gray know you are here," she said and then disappeared into his office.

"Claire," Mr. Lucas said, turning his back to the two officers and whispering to me. "When I see you safely into this office, my assignment will be complete and I have to head back to the mainland. I don't know what you're here for or what's going on in your life, but I just want you to know if you need anything, ever, just call." He reached into his jacket and pulled out a business card. It was the plainest business card I had ever seen, all white with just the name "Lucas" in the middle and his number underneath.

I took the card, my face smiling with gratitude. That kind gesture somehow gave me reassurance that everything was going to be ok. I shook his hand. "Thank you so much Mr. Lucas. I really mean it."

The office door opening caught our attention. Lt. General Gray came out with the secretary behind him.

I was surprised to see him, having just put two and two together, that he was the same General that had visited me over the weekend at Campbell. How did I not catch that and how did he get here so fast? I thought he was from Washington. Isn't that what General Collins had said?

I stood at attention with the two officers, while Lt. General Gray took my paperwork from Lucas, signed a form, and then shook hands. He put us at ease and invited us into his office. I followed them, but not before giving Lucas a final nod. He smiled and nodded back then headed to the door. I wondered what mission he was headed to next.

SEVENTEEN

WE WERE WELCOMED to sit in the three chairs across the desk from Lt. Gen. Gray.

I suddenly felt alone sitting there with these two guys who obviously wanted nothing to do with me, though they didn't know my story, or why I was even there. To them I was just an enlisted man who was being given preferential treatment they thought I did not deserve. I didn't care though. A year ago I would have cared and fretted over what they thought about me, but not anymore. One of the great things about maturing and going through all I had faced the past two years, was not caring what people thought about me. I don't mean that in a bad way. I care about who I am, but if I've done all I can to be the best person I can be and that's still not enough, I simply don't care. I guess I just mean to say that I am who I am and that's good enough. So anyways, no sweat off my brow if they didn't want to deal with me.

"Airman Haley, it's so nice to see you again," Lt. General Gray smiled at me. "We're so excited to have you here at Hickam."

I saw the older officer shift uncomfortably in his chair, folding his arms across his chest.

"Thank you Lt. Gen. Gray. I'm so excited to be a part of Hickam," I said.

"How was your journey here?" he asked, sitting at his desk.

"It was ok. I've never flown for that long before." I paused for a moment, biting my lower lip, making sure I hadn't given anything away. Flying for me usually meant minus the plane. Lt. General caught my hesitation and smirked at me, shaking his head.

"Well, I'm glad you made it safely. Perhaps we should get you in the air a little more while you're here." He winked at me and I took that to mean, *maybe* I would get to fly here. Wishful thinking.

Lt. General Gray picked up a folder from his desk. "Ok Captain Crew, Airman Haley will be in your company during her tenure here."

"Yes Sir," the Captain said, staring straight ahead, arms still folded and his smugness, so hard to ignore.

I looked over at him, waiting for him to acknowledge me, but he didn't even glance my way. I directed my attention back to Lt. Gen. Gray, who cleared his throat in the uneasiness of the moment.

"Um, so Airman Haley, Captain Crew is one of our top leaders here at Hickam," he explained, almost as if to apologize for Crew's coldness. "He runs a tight ship at his special units company and we think you'll be a fine addition there."

I smiled slightly and raised an eyebrow at Lt. Gen. Gray, letting him know that was a nice try, but I knew I clearly was not wanted. He smiled at me and continued on, pointing at the other officer.

"I know you've met Major Wang, but just so you know, he is the lead doctor here at Tripler Medical Center." I glanced at Major Wang, who offered me a somewhat smile and a nod. "He will be doing regular check ups on you in Dr. York's absence." Major Yang once again smiled and nodded in my direction. "So Haley's assignment with us is simple. She is an airman first and is to follow all the rules and directions of your unit, however, there are some special instructions here, as her schedule will differ from time to time."

Lt. General Gray handed each of us a small packet to view and continued with his directions. "As you can see on page two, there are some things that differ from regular airmen. For example, if she needs a pass off the base, it must be cleared with you Capt. Crew, and she must be accompanied at all times." He stood up and walked around to the front of his desk, leaning against it. "So does anyone have questions or remarks?"

I stared at him unsure of what to say, much less ask. Did these guys know anything about me? I didn't want to say too much and give myself away. Luckily, Captain Crew spoke up.

"Well, Airman Haley, like Lt. General said, I run a tight ship. We welcome any personnel who are willing to work hard and be a team player. Our unit specializes in missions, not common to other companies, so it's imperative that you pay attention, make good decisions, and follow the rules. I'm interested to see how you will contribute to our team and the talents that placed you in my company."

In other words, he was completely unaware of my flying powers and why I was there. I sensed he knew there was a government secret surrounding me and was offended he knew nothing about it. What do I say to that? I managed an "I will do my best, Sir," and left it there.

Lt. General Gray looked over at Major Wang, who took that as his cue to greet me in his thick Korean accent. "Aiman Haley, welcome to Hickam. I am Senior Officer at Tripler Medical and I will be making sure you stay healthy and in good shape during your stay here at Hickam." He again smiled and bowed slightly at me and in return I did the same.

"Ok Gentlemen," Lt. Gen.Gray said, leaning off his desk. "Thank you for picking up Airman Haley for me. Captain Crew, I will be sending her over as soon as we finish up some things here."

He showed them both to the door, while I remained in my seat, rubbing a small scuff off my overly polished combat boots. My uniform suddenly felt very heavy, after having traveled in it for the last day and a half and my head hurt a little from the heavy bun I had my long hair wrapped in. Captain Crew turned and mumbled something to Lt. Gen. Gray, who in return nodded and patted him on the back in reassurance. He closed the door and joined me, sitting in the seat Capt. Crew had just occupied.

Maybe I looked tired or maybe he just felt sorry for me, but something prompted him to say, "Claire, I know it's not easy leaving your family and coming here alone, especially after all you've been through the last two years, but we're going to do everything to make your stay with us a good one."

I nodded my head quietly. "Thank you Lt. Gen. Gray. I really appreciate that." I paused for a moment. "May I ask what they think I'm here for, because obviously they have no idea what's going on with me."

He sighed, "I know, Claire...and I know that would make things easier, but we have to keep this a government secret for as long as we can. At least until we can figure out what's going on...but more importantly for your safety."

"I understand, but do you think all of this is necessary? Like me not being able to leave base without an escort?"

"Of course. We wouldn't even have you here if we didn't think there was a threat...which is why you're in Captain Crew's unit. I know he's a bit harsh, but I can tell you one thing, with that unit, you will be safe at all times. They don't mess around."

"Do they have any idea that I'm a 'top government

secret'?" I asked a bit embarrassed by the term.

Lt. General dropped his voice a little. "Well, no, but we have a lot of government secrets floating around out there and the world is a better place because they are just that...secrets."

I nodded knowingly, curious to know what governmental secret compared to me. Aliens maybe? I know that sounds conceited, but I was pretty cool.

"Ok, so just a few things," he said standing up and grabbing my folder. "Under no circumstances are you to even hint of your power. Everyone is being told you are here for hand to hand combat training, which you will receive, but that's all they need to know. If they prod, and they will, you tell them you're just following orders. Secondly, you are to stay out of the sky. No flying, Claire."

I cringed and shifted in my seat. "Will I get any flying time?"

"For experimental purposes only. Just to monitor any changes."

"Lt. General, with all due respect, do you have any idea what it's like to have something as incredible as this and never get to use it?"

He nodded, agreeing with me. "I can only imagine how annoying that would be. I get it. I'm a jet pilot...but Claire," his eyes twinkled, "we won't have eyes on you all the time, you know."

I smiled, reading between the lines. Maybe Hickam wouldn't be too terrible a place after all.

EIGHTEEN

LT. GENERAL GRAY drove me to my barracks at the 180th Special Forces Unit, pointing out various restaurants and stores along the way. We stopped in front of a tan building with tall palm trees in front and to my surprise, he escorted me inside. Airman mingled around the front and inside and immediately froze, standing at attention as we walked by.

"Sometimes I like to drop in, just to meet my airmen," he explained.

"That's so nice," I replied. "I'm sure they appreciate that."

"At ease gentlemen," he commanded in his deep voice as we entered an office just inside the building. He looked at one officer in particular. "Sgt. Mancuso, this is Airman Haley. I'm sure Captain Crew has told you about her arrival."

"Yes Sir, Lt. General. We have her room all ready."

Lt. General handed Sgt. Mancuso my folder. "All of her information is in here.

I will be back tomorrow morning to discuss her assignment further with you and Crew. I would stay longer, but I have an aggravated wife who is already upset with my absence this whole weekend and I need to make it home for dinner."

"Yes Sir," Mancuso chuckled.

I felt a pang of guilt, knowing that absence included me. Lt. General had flown to Campbell Friday, met with my family Saturday, then jetted back here right after. I'm sure he was as exhausted as I was.

He turned to me. "Alright Haley. If you need anything, anything at all, you know where to find me."

"Yes Sir," I said, giving one final salute. "Thank you Lt. General, Sir."

"Take care of this one," he called over his shoulder to the other airmen as he headed out of the building.

"Yes Sir!" a group of voices called out in unison.

I watched him leave, then turned around to face all eight pairs of eyes in the room staring me down, full of curiosity. I was suddenly aware of how much I didn't blend with this group. They came in all nationalities, but had the same thing in common; their size. These guys looked like the O-line for the Titans.

Sgt. Mancuso finally spoke. "All right Haley, grab your gear. I'll show you to your room."

I grabbed my heavy duffle and flung it over my shoulder, almost falling as the weight of the bag pulled me backwards. It took all the strength I had to get it over and I muffled a grunt not wanting these guys to think I was a wimp by any means. It was so important to me to fit in and carry my weight in any situation I found myself in, and I obviously had a lot of weight to carry here.

Sgt. Mancuso tucked a grin between his lips and turned to me. "Follow me, Haley."

We walked down the hallway to a door where a staircase wound its way up 4 flights of stairs. "We're on the very top," he said almost apologetically.

"No elevator?" I asked, but immediately regretted it. *"Wimp status already, Claire,"* I lectured myself inwardly.

"Yes, but it's for officers only. No worries though, it'll be good for your leg endurance."

"Oh, I agree," I smiled.

Man oh man was he right about the leg endurance thing. By the time we got to the 4th floor, I was feeling it, especially carrying my 20 pound duffle and backpack. I paced my breath, so he couldn't hear my heavy breathing. At last we hit the final step on the fourth floor, my calves feeling like they were on fire. I could have sworn after all the PT hours I put in, I was in better shape than this.

"So where are you from?" he asked as we walked down the hallway.

"Ft. Campbell."

"Campbell? Isn't that an army base?"

"Yes, but they have a small Air Force company stationed there also."

He turned and looked at me over his shoulder. "Oh really? Any special ops like us?"

Lt. General's warning echoed through my thoughts. I had to be careful what I said. "Umm, not that I'm aware of." *What was it Lt. General told me to say?* "They just gave me orders to come here, so I did." Yikes. That sounded out of place and I could tell from Mancuso's weird glance at me, he agreed.

"Ok, so here we are," he said sliding a key into my door, the last one at the end of the hall. "You're in luck, because this is an officer's floor only. They put you up here because...because I guess there's no more rooms available." He pointed behind us, "That's my room across the hall if you need anything."

I walked into my room and gasped quietly at the view before me. A small, but still spacious room, with a conjoined kitchenette, living room, and bed cozied together to make a perfect living space. My bed, that sat close to a sliding glass door, opened up to a tiny deck that barely fit a couple of chairs. Just beyond that, I could see the waters of the Pacific Ocean rolling toward the coast, their roar relaxing me immediately.

"Beautiful, right?"

I had almost forgotten Mancuso was still there.

"Yes Sir," I said. "Thank you, Sgt. Mancuso. I know I don't deserve this room, but I'm very grateful."

Sgt. Mancuso looked at me and nodded, almost as

if he seemed surprised by my gratitude. "No problem, Haley. Dinner is at 1800. It's two buildings south of here. It's olive green. You can't miss it."

"Yes Sir."

He put the key on the kitchen counter and left. I opened the slider to the sound of waves crashing and seagulls singing. The smell of salt water filled my room and I sat on the bed to get my hot boots off. I pulled off my socks and uniform and left on nothing but my cami and boxer shorts. The bed squeaked as I unrolled my sheets and pillows and finally laid down. I had about 45 minutes before dinner, and the drowsiness from the past 24 hours was beginning to envelop me. The soft bed melted around me and I drifted off into the calmest sleep I had in weeks.

A vibrating sound in my ear woke me at once. I looked around the almost dark, unfamiliar room, unsure of where I was. Some hotel on vacation? The sound of waves crashing and the breeze wisping through the trees outside brought me back to my new reality; Hickam. Somewhere in the distance, I could hear a jet, its engines screaming on final approach. My phone vibrated again and I fumbled in the darkness trying to find it, at last pulling it from underneath my pillow. I looked at the time, 11:30 pm. I had been asleep for 5 hours.

"Johnny?" I answered in my drowsiness.

"Claire!" I heard his sweet voice exclaim. "I've been texting and calling. Are you ok?"

I rubbed my eyes. I was so tired I could easily fall right back to sleep. "I'm so sorry, mister. I got here and fell asleep. I feel so tired, and on top of that, I left my phone on vibrate."

"It's ok," he reassured me. "I was just worried about you."

"Johnny, hold on one second." I sat up and scooted over to a dark silhouette I could tell was a lamp, and slid my hand up the base in search of the switch and clicked it on. The room filled with a warm soft glow. "I had to turn the light on," I explained.

"So how did everything go?" he asked.

"It was ok. Remember Lt. General Gray from the meeting Saturday?"

"Yeah."

"Well, he's here. I had a meeting with him today. I guess he's the General of this base."

"Oh wow, they didn't mention that."

I sighed. "I know. I guess that's why they sent me here. I can really be under their eye now."

"Well, just remember, it's only for a season," he reassured me.

"I guess, but I miss you so much already."

"I miss you too, Claire Bear."

It was quiet for a moment. I was so tired and my tummy silently growled at me for having neglected it the last couple of days. Come to think of it, I hadn't eaten since that slice of pizza I had on Saturday night and it was already late Monday night.

"Claire?" Johnny's voice trembled over the phone. "Claire, I have to tell you something."

My heart dropped and my tired eyes popped open. All thoughts of sleeplessness and hunger left immediately. Johnny never trembled at anything. He was the most brave person I had ever known, so for him to be bothered, it had to be something significant.

"Ok," I answered quietly.

"I didn't want to tell you this over the phone, but with everything happening to you so quickly this weekend...I just thought the timing would be bad."

"Ok," I answered again, this time my voice being the one to tremble.

"Claire, we're not breaking up," Johnny smiled through his voice.

I breathed a sigh of relief. I always thought that's where these conversations were going, and this time I would definitely deserve it after what I put him through.

"I'm sorry," I laughed nervously.

"It's ok," he replied. I heard him gulp, then "Claire, I got orders last week for deployment."

"Deployment?" I repeated, trying to catch my breath.
"Yes."

"To Germany? To...to Sinai?" We had always talked about one of those being a possibility, but since everything had gone down with my flying power, I was pretty much assured Johnny would be staying at Campbell with me.

"No," he said, clearing his throat. "Afghanistan."

"No," I gasped. "No, Johnny...you're...you're supposed to be here with me."

"I have to go, Claire," he interrupted softly. "I can't stay here where it's safe, while my whole company goes. It's not fair. What kind of soldier would that make me?"

"But...but I need you," I argued, a knot rising in my throat. "I'm going to be back home in a couple of weeks and I'll need you there with me."

"Claire, you're safe where you are. They've assigned you to one of the toughest units anywhere, and...and I'm sorry, but you're not going to be back in a couple of weeks. You'll be there for a while and that makes me feel better about leaving you."

I was dumbfounded. All kinds of emotions filled my heart. Sadness, loneliness, betrayal, and a bit of bitterness. Tears flooded my very tired eyes. How could he do this to me and how did he know I would be here for a while? Was this pre-planned? Had he been talking to someone behind my back? Maybe the bridge accident was just an excuse to get me out of Campbell, so he could deploy.

"Claire?" I didn't answer. I had no words to say. "Come on, sweetness. You know this is something I can't help."

Ok, maybe I did have a few words to say. "Johnny, how do you know I'll be here for a while?" I asked. "Was this pre-planned? You guys sent me here so you can deploy?"

"Claire, you know that's not true," Johnny replied, his voice more firm. "You know I've never kept a secret from you."

Ok, that was an obvious stab at me for keeping my flying power a secret from him for so long.

"You know I had no choice with that," I almost whispered. "I was protecting you."

"No choice with what?"

"Nevermind." I sighed. He knew exactly what I was talking about.

"Claire, please don't be mad at me."

I rubbed my eyes that were quickly filling with tears again. "When do you leave?" I asked as they began to fall freely down my flushed cheeks.

"Friday."

"So soon?" I gasped.

"Yeah. I'm going ahead of everyone else for some pre-training at Benning."

"What about Shawn? Isn't he going with you?"

"Well yeah, but he won't come until after Labor Day."

"Does Alicia know?"

"He's telling her this weekend."

I buried my eyes in my hands and sobbed, not caring if Johnny heard me. Normally I would hide any emotions that would make him feel bad, but not this time. I wanted him to feel the hurt and the pain I felt. Johnny was my world and I shuddered at the thought of losing him. He filled a hole in my life that had been empty since my dad died and already I was feeling that hole empty out again.

"Claire, it's only for 7 months," he tried to reassure me. "I'll be back before next spring."

I couldn't answer. I cried even more, as I felt the sting of loss that took me back to the death of my dad.

"Claire...listen to me. I'm not leaving you. I'm going to do this deployment while you're away. Don't you see? This is a good thing. If I'm going to deploy, I want to go while you're gone, while I know you are safe and I don't have to worry about you."

We were quiet again. I felt so drained emotionally. I understood Johnny's reasoning and why he felt he couldn't tell me, but at the same time, here I sat a whole country away with no chance of saying goodbye properly. Sometimes in his quest to protect me, he forgets that I really am a strong person.

I dried my tears and tried to push away the pouting from my voice. "I understand where you're coming from, but we agreed to no more secrets. You've obviously known about this for a while."

"I know. I'm sorry. I just didn't know what was going to happen for sure," he said quietly.

I felt my heart soften. I knew Johnny really cared about me and worried about my safety, just as much as I worried about his.

"I wish I were in the States," I said, "because I don't care what anyone says, I would fly myself home so I could see you before Friday."

Johnny laughed, "I wish you could."

I blew my nose, sounding like a distressed foghorn.

"Did you blow out a lung, there?" he asked.

I giggled at him. He was so funny.

"I love you, Claire. I promise no more secrets, no matter what."

"I love you too, Johnny. You better keep me up to date on everything that's happening over there. I want a text everyday. I mean it."

"Well, that goes for you too, Missy. None of this 'my phone was on vibrate or...or...I fell asleep stuff."

"Yes Sir." I laughed.

We talked for over an hour, then finally hung up. I sat in the loneliness of the dim room listening to my tummy growl again, but I didn't care. I brushed my teeth and went to bed. Tomorrow I would start a new beginning, in a new place, with new people, and my heart sank at the thought of it. I wanted to go home.

NINETEEN

FIVE A.M. CAME all too quickly the next day. I scurried to get up and shower and throw on my PT uniform, which was a basic light gray tee and navy blue shorts. Staring in the mirror, I attempted to give myself a pep talk.

"Ok Claire, you got this," I said, pulling my long curls into a tight bun and securing my hat with two bobby pins. "These guys are some of the toughest in the Air Force, but you know what? They can't fly."

Outside on the back lawn I lined up with 50 of my fellow airmen in formation as the sun began to rise over the east side of the building. It was only 5:30 and already a balmy 80 degrees.

I was surprised to see Capt. Crew there and so early. Usually a high ranking officer like him never showed up to PT. He walked between us, every now and then stopping to commend someone or remind them of where they were lacking.

He never once raised his voice, but his brazen stare was enough to make one not repeat the same mistake again.

When at last he reached my row, my heart skipped a beat on his approach. Just as I thought he would, he paused in front of me, his stare icy and cold.

"Think you can keep up with these guys, Haley?" he asked so that no one else heard.

"Yes Sir, Captain Crew," I replied.

Captain Crew stepped back and spoke louder so everyone around could hear this time. "I can't hear you in that squeaky mouse of a voice, Haley. I asked if you can keep up with these boys?"

"Yes Sir, Captain Sir!" I almost yelled.

"Well, I hope your PT skills are stronger than your voice."

I heard a couple of stifled giggles around me. My body tensed in the moment, not from embarrassment, but from pure anger. I have this thing about me, that if someone makes me feel like I can't accomplish something, that makes me want to conquer it even more. It makes me irritated in a good way, because from that irritation comes determination and usually I can finish anything I put my mind to.

It's a great motivational push for me and little did I know how much I was going to need it on this morning.

We started with typical PT training: push ups, planks, lunges, and chin ups. I was proud of myself for being able to keep up, but then we moved into some training I had never done before.

"Alright, grab a log and get into line!" Mancuso ordered us. I joined everyone in grabbing logs from a pile of wood set on the side of a storage shed. The logs were well worn, almost smooth from being carried so many times before and heavy, very heavy.

"Alright, overhead!" he yelled. Everyone lifted the logs above their heads and I followed suit. "Let's go!"

We began in a slow jog that led us between the row of barracks and down a narrow path that combined our two lines into one. Palm trees swayed overhead and twice I almost lost my footing on the uneven ground. A few minutes later, the trees parted and before us stretched a perfect white sandy beach that seemed to go on forever.

Running on the ground was challenging enough, but in the sand and carrying the log...I can't even tell you how hard that was. Every now and then Mancuso would order us "down" and we would bring the log in front of us for a moment's rest, before it was ordered up again. My arms and shoulders burned. Muscles that I didn't even know I had felt like they were on fire.

We ran for what seemed like forever, at last turning around at a lighthouse surrounded by uneven, jagged rock.

"Down!" Mancuso ordered again.

I brought the log in front of me, my body weight lunging forward with it, just as my sneaker slipped on a slimy, wet rock. A sharp pain ripped through my left leg as the rock sliced my bare skin.

I clenched my teeth together, while scolding myself. *"Seriously Claire. What the heck?"* I looked down at a stream of blood running down my leg and onto my white ankle sock, as the other airmen continued a path around me. I jumped up immediately and grabbed my log that had rolled down the rock and got back into formation. How was I going to make it back? I had barely made it here and now the cut on my leg stung in the thick salt water air. I began to fall behind in formation. Before I knew it, I was last in line and even then, a few empty feet behind.

"It's fine, Claire," I quietly cheered myself on. "Just don't quit."

Twenty minutes later we arrived back at the barracks, me still trailing pretty far behind. By the time I reached the lawn, the other airmen were catching their breath, some of them laying on the ground or sitting against the building in the shade.

Mancuso and Captain Crew stopped their conversation to watch me run to the shed and drop my log. I tried to walk as normal as I could with my chin up. There was no way I was going to let these guys see me down.

"You ok there, Haley?" Mancuso asked with a smirk.

"Just fine, Sergeant," I said, passing them without even a glance. I was completely drenched in sweat and walked to the water fountain to clean up my leg as best as I could. The cold water felt amazing as it cleaned out the salt water and sand from my cut.

"You should probably take that to the medic station before it gets infected," I heard a nasally voice above me. I looked up from my crouched position to see a skinny, Asian guy, no taller than me, staring down through his thick bottle glasses.

I stood up and looked at him, a little surprised to see him there. No offense to him, but if he was in this company, he stuck out like a sore thumb, just like me.

"Are you…?" I started to ask pointing at the rest of the guys behind us.

"Yes, I'm in this company" he answered before I could finish. "Shocker right?"

"Well…" I started to try to explain myself a little embarrassed, but he interrupted again.

"I could think the same about you," he said with one eyebrow cocked in curiosity and his arms folded across his chest. "What are you doing here? I've never seen a girl here before."

I blinked in surprise at his forwardness. "I'm…I'm just here because this is where I've been assigned to be."

He shifted his body to the other leg, arms still folded, and rolled his eyes like he didn't believe me. I didn't blame him. I wouldn't believe me either.

"Nice try, Airman Haley."

"Thanks Airman…" I looked at his name patch. "Zhao."

He smiled at me. "Good first try. Most people butcher it. Come on, us undesirables have to stick together."

I followed him down the sidewalk. "What about

formation?"

"Oh we're done," he reassured me. "They were dismissed for breakfast before you got back."

"Oh," I said, clenching my teeth in embarrassment.

"Don't stress it. You finished. That's what counts."

Zhao led me to a small white building at the end of the sidewalk. A weathered sign that read "Medic" hung above the chipped up, salt worn, red wooden door. This place could definitely use a fresh coat of paint. The OCD person in me wanted to grab a sander and repaint it a fresh red, the way it should be.

We walked inside where Zhao introduced me to the medic on duty, Sgt. Hunley.

"You're in the 180th?" he asked, somewhat surprised.

"Yes Sir!" I answered as confidently as I could.

"She's with me," Zhao snorted when he laughed. "Birds of a feather…"

If Zhao wasn't so friendly, I would almost think he was making fun of me, but instead I laughed with them.

"Alright Haley, you're good," Sgt. Hunley said after applying the last butterfly bandage.

"Thank you Sgt. Hunley. I didn't think it was that big of a deal, but Zhao insisted."

"Well, I'm glad you stopped by. Bacteria on those rocks are nothing to scoff at."

I shook his hand and thanked him once more. Zhao led me outside and down the path to the green building that was the chow hall, where I was supposed to show up to last night for dinner. Talking to him was so easy and I enjoyed hearing all about his history, as I hungrily scarfed down the eggs, bacon, and toast we were served.

"Wow Haley. Starve much?" he teased me, giving me his last piece of toast.

"I haven't eaten in two days," I tried to explain between bites.

So Zhao was originally from Kyoto, Japan, and his family had emigrated to the states when he was just five years old. His dad was a brilliant physicist who worked in Washington for the government and then in Texas for NASA.

"Yeah, so the US offered my dad a job and the next thing I knew, we became US citizens and were standing in a courtroom taking the Oath of Allegiance. My mom and dad were so happy. I remember my mom couldn't stop crying."

"That's so awesome," I smiled at him. "So how did you end up here?"

"Well, I was at Yale studying aeronautics, when I got a call requesting I use my degree in the Air Force after graduating. I got stationed in Texas, but then a couple of months ago they suddenly changed my orders and brought me here."

My eyes got big. "You have an aeronautics degree from Yale?" I gasped.

"Yep," he replied like it was no big deal. "So here I am with my degree, stationed in Hawaii, in a company that trains in hand to hand combat," he shrugged. "Makes no sense."

I stared at him for a moment, the pieces of his puzzle falling into place, at least for me. I began to feel sick to my stomach. It was very clear to me why Zhao was here. For me.

"What?" he asked, snapping me out of my glare.

"Oh nothing," I answered. "I just have a feeling we'll be seeing a lot of each other."

Zhao wrinkled his nose in bewilderment. "Why do you say that?"

I bit my lip realizing I probably shouldn't have said that. "Ummm...well, just because of our interests. I have some flight experience." *Shut up, Claire... I warned myself.*

"Oh really? What kind?"

To my relief, the breakfast bell rang and we headed outside with the rest of the guys. I didn't want to answer his last question.

"Well Haley, I'll catch you at dinner tonight."

"Where are you going?" I asked, sad to be parting with my only friend.

"Aeronautics stuff," he smiled and headed in the opposite direction.

TWENTY

I SPENT THE rest of the week doing morning PT and then some mundane tasks like power spraying sidewalks, always under the watchful eye of Sgt. Mancuso and sometimes Capt. Crew himself. Nights were spent alone in my room on the phone with either my family, Alicia, or Johnny. By this time Shawn had told Alicia he was being deployed and we talked for a good hour on the phone consoling each other the best we could.

On Friday afternoon Sgt. Mancuso approached me as I hung up the hose for the power sprayer in the shed.

"Haley, grab your purse or whatever it is you carry. I'm going to take you off base and show you around so you can get anything you may need."

Fifteen minutes later I hopped into Mancuso's truck and we headed off base.

"Where are we going?" I asked, curious as to what stores they had here.

"Walmart," he answered to my surprise.

"You guys have Walmart here?" I almost laughed.

"Claire, there's a Walmart everywhere," he smiled.

That's the first time I had ever heard him use my first name and the first time I had ever seen a smile. Maybe he wasn't as grumpy as I thought.

At Walmart we split up. I grabbed my stuff as quickly as possible, knowing he wouldn't be too long. I needed all new stuff, from a throw blanket to bathroom necessities. I also grabbed some lounge clothes and new flip flops and finally some snack items. Luckily, he only had to wait for me a few minutes.

"That was fast," he laughed. "I figured we would be here a while."

"I've learned to be quick," I smiled. "My boyfriend hates waiting too."

We grabbed tacos to go, since we had both missed dinner and on the way home Mancuso asked all about my family, Ft. Campbell, and Johnny. I noticed he was very careful to not ask me about the how or why I was there and for that I was truly grateful.

I sat alone in my room that night picnicking on my bed, eating my tacos and watching "Sleepless in Seattle." The barracks was eerily quiet. It was Friday night and everyone had gone off base, I assumed. My slider door was open, allowing the warm salt water air to blow through the room. It was equally as quiet outside, except the constant sound of waves crashing and whisping of the palm tree branches.

Johnny's face ran through my thoughts and I imagined where he was and what he was doing as he left Campbell tonight for deployment. I hadn't heard from him since last night and he said the chances of me hearing from him over the weekend were slim to none, but around 11 pm my text dinged. To my delight Johnny's name popped up.

"Hey there Claire Bear."

"Hi my Johnny! I wasn't expecting to hear from you!"

"I have a layover for a few minutes, so I just wanted to text you and let you know I'm thinking about you. I love and miss you so much."

Oh wow. He was so sweet to me.

"I love and miss you too Johnny. So much."

"Are you doing ok? Is everyone treating you ok?"

"Yes. They're fine. I'm ok."

I wanted to tell him how depressed and homesick I was, but I didn't dare add to the stress I'm sure he was already feeling.

"This is just a season, Claire. It will be over before you know it."

That's the thing about Johnny. He can pick up on my mood, even through texting. It's just too crazy.

"I know it is. I can't wait to see you again, Mister."

We said goodbye. I knew it would be a while before I would hear from him again for real this time and a dark cloud formed over my heart. I looked down at my tat that was glowing a bright pink. I hadn't seen it glow in a while. When I wasn't able to fly, it stayed a dull pink and gray.

I walked over to the small balcony and breathed in the fresh air. Hawaii smelled amazing. The back field of the barracks was empty and I could see everything thanks to the bright moon. Its white glow illuminated the billowing clouds rolling in against the ebony sky above the ocean.

I wanted to fly so bad. "Don't do it, Claire," I warned myself, biting my lip and grasping the balcony rail, as if that would keep me on the ground. Maybe it would be ok if I just flew to the roof. I overheard someone say the view from there was incredible.

I threw on my Adidas and a frumpy beach tee over my cami. The back training field was still quiet and empty. I slid my balcony door shut, checked the area one more time, and flew to the top of the building, guiding myself cautiously over the wall.

The roof was empty except for a few deck chairs and a door that led to the stairs. I layed back in one of the chairs and took in my favorite scenery ever; the sky. The stars twinkled above me, the exact same stars that hung above Clarksville tonight. I missed home and my family terribly. It had only been a week since I left, but it felt like forever.

A shooting star streaked high above and my Saturn rings glowed even brighter.

Hmmm...maybe I could just fly to that lighthouse we'd been running around all week. It wasn't too far away, so it wouldn't be like I was flying a long distance. I walked over to the edge of the building, scanning the area for any eyes and when I felt I was safe, jumped into the dark sky. The breeze coming off the water was so calming. I forgot all of my troubles as I rose high above the Pacific to get safely out of sight.

Soon the lighthouse flashed majestically below, as the foamy waves slammed into the splintering rocks around it. Cautiously descending from my height of 300 feet, I landed softly on the slanted roof of the lighthouse.

"*This is so cool!*" I thought, as I situated myself on the rough tiles facing the ocean. "*Claire, you're a lucky girl.*"

The roof of the old lighthouse reminded me of the courthouse in Clarksville, where I used to sit on summer nights like these and watch the sparkling traffic lights of the bustling city move around in complete oblivion to my presence there. Once again my heart ached for home, but if I was going to be anywhere else in the world, I was so blessed to be here. I leaned back against the steep roof that acted as a lounge chair, turned on Frank Sinatra, and let his song "Summerwind" fill my ears. Before I knew it, thirty minutes had flown by quickly in this magical space. My tattoo glowed in bright pink happiness, almost as if to say "thank you" for the flight tonight.

Suddenly, a siren cut through the night air, startling

me out of my serenity. I looked into the darkness and saw a boat, lights flashing, headed out into the ocean. Irresistible curiosity consumed me. Some people would call it nosiness instead, but it's not all completely my fault. I partially blame my sweet mother for it. When we were little and out and about, she would follow cop cars and ambulances, curious to know where they were going. Call us weird, but we enjoyed it, so not wanting to break tradition, I just had to follow that boat.

I dove off the light house and into the sky in hot pursuit of the boat. I very quickly caught them, my speed intimidating to even the most advanced military aircraft. I had never fully tested my limits out of fear of fainting, but in Houston I was tested in the desert, under the cover of night. Commander Whitley put some kind of speed device on me and I had reached 150 knots without breathing difficulty or dizziness.

We were about 10 minutes into the journey when a bright white flare shot into the distance lighting up the western sky.

I watched in fascination as the boat approached a smaller vessel that had capsized. A small raft had been deployed and was sitting not far from the bottom up boat, rocking on the waves. Dozens of white packages floated around the area, obviously drugs of some sort. The Coast Guard shined a bright light on the raft ordering all five occupants to put their hands in the air.

I sat high above the Coast Guard boat, my usual Indian style position, watching in awe. This was better than a movie!

Within 10 minutes the Coast Guard had the men handcuffed and secured on the boat. I shot higher into the air thrilled with my mini show tonight. The Coast Guard was incredible! What a brave job to have.

I looked at my watch. 1 am. Not ready to go back, I looked around curious to see if there were any whales out. My experience with the one in Florida was exhilarating and I wanted that rush again.

I flew down to the surface of the water, skimming my hands on the warm tide, its mist covering me. In the distance waves breaking against something caught my attention. To be safe, I soared higher to see what it was. A small island appeared, it's black silhouette standing out against the diamond ocean.

I cautiously landed on the soft white sand and looked around. From the air the island appeared to be no bigger than two miles long and maybe a mile wide. The south side was more open vegetation and white sandy beaches, while the north side looked like a tropical forest. I couldn't be too sure because of the darkness, but to my delight it seemed to be uninhabited.

I took off my shoes and walked the sandy beach, the white foamy waves washing over my feet. The bright moon shone directly overhead and the sounds of nature were unlike anything I had ever heard before. In the distance an unknown bird cawed and something that sounded like a soft whistle came streaming out of the forest.

Normally, I would have been nervous about the

unknown in the darkness around me, but the ability to rocket out of any situation made me fearless.

I breathed in the fresh air, my face moist from the spray of the ocean. This was now my island and I made plans in my mind to spend as much free time here as I could. I took out my phone and found myself on the longitude and latitude app and took a screenshot so I could find my way back. Alicia and Kass were never going to believe this.

Before I knew it, the moon had moved further to the west and the clock on my phone read 3 am. I knew I had better get back before anyone noticed or the sun began to rise.

I put my phone in my back pocket, grabbed my shoes, and jumped into the night air. I didn't realize it, but I had wandered about an hour from the base. Finding my way back was a little difficult, but I used other islands as markers and breathed a sigh of relief when the lighthouse flashed in the distance.

What an incredible night. Hawaii was growing on me.

TWENTY-ONE

MONDAY MORNING, AFTER another torturous log hike, I stood at the fountain rubbing my raw hands under the cool water as inconspicuous as I could.

"They'll eventually harden and you won't feel it as much," Zhao encouraged me.

"Oh, I'm fine. They're just sweaty," I shrugged nonchalantly.

Zhao laughed at my obvious lie. "Come on, Claire. You're with me today."

"What? Are you sure? I thought Sgt. Mancuso said I would be on the power sprayer again."

"Overrided," Zhao said, nodding behind him.

I looked to where he was pointing. Lt. General Gray stood in the shade of a palm tree talking to Sgt. Mancuso. They both looked and waved us over. Zhao and I immediately went to them and stood at attention.

"Airman Haley, Airman Zhao at ease," he instructed us. "You guys ready to go?"

"Yes Sir," we said in unison, though I had no idea where we were going.

We followed Lt. General to the front of the barracks and into an unmarked government vehicle.

"The Shack," Lt. General instructed the driver.

I looked over at Zhao and raised my eyebrows to question where we were going. He in return just smiled knowingly back at me.

We left the base and followed a curving road that led up the coast, about 20 minutes away. Along the way the Lt. General questioned us about how we were adjusting to Hawaii and how everyone was treating us. Of course Zhao and I didn't dare complain. What good would it do anyway?

The driver turned west into a brick road that led up to a gate. A large red sign hung on the gate that read:

RESTRICTED FACILITY
UNITED STATES AIR FORCE

The guard looked into the vehicle at Lt. General Gray and immediately saluted, then ordered the gate open. A large building awaited us at the end of the palm tree lined driveway. It definitely didn't look like a shack to me.

Zhao and I climbed out of the vehicle and followed Lt. General into a spacious foyer and down a hallway. This building almost reminded me of an old high school, but much nicer. I gasped quietly when we reached another large foyer in the backside of the building. A two story wall of glass windows revealed some of the most beautiful plants I had ever seen outside. The light green painted walls added to the feel of an inside jungle.

Just outside the door, we followed a sidewalk that snaked through the lush vegetation and at the end of the path, a wooden bamboo themed building appeared.

"Ohhhh...the Shack. I get it now," I thought to myself.

The door of the building creaked open and an intimidating looking man with salt and pepper hair greeted us with a bow and a kind smile, under his furry beard. Zhao and Lt. General returned his bow and we followed him inside.

"Airman Haley, I would like for you to meet Professor Braulio Corral. He will be teaching you everything you need to know. You're a bit too wimpy for the talents you possess and you need some fighting skills. Professor Corral will help you get to level."

I nodded and smiled, despite his obvious insult and looked around the large room. Everything I need to know as far as what goes? From the looks of it, this was like a Karate dojo. Red, white, and blue mats lined the floor and a large, well worn punching bag hung in the corner. Mirrors lined one side of the bamboo walls and dozens of trophies and medals filled a sparkling glass case on the other.

"Professor Corral excels in knitting," Zhao smirked at

me.

"Watch it Zhao," Lt. General smiled, shaking his head, while Professor Corral chuckled. "Alright you guys. You'll return on the shuttle." He looked over at me, "Learn something, Claire."

"Yes Sir," I said shyly, as I watched him walk out the door.

Professor Corral had us both sit on the mat and he joined us. "Hello, like Lt. General said, my name is Braulio (bra-lee-o) Corral, but you can call me Professor B. I'm excited to have you both here today. I have the utmost respect for those who serve our country. If I can show you something today that will help you when you are in harm's way, it would truly be an honor. "

I knew right away that I would like Professor B. I could see and feel that he was very confident, but not arrogant. There was a calm about him and strangely, he made me feel a little more relaxed.

Professor B then gave us a history lesson in the incredible world of his craft, Brazilian Jiu Jitsu. He explained how it was created to help the smaller person defend himself against a stronger and larger attacker and that fit Zhao and I to a T. He further explained that Brazilian Jiu Jitsu is the fight that begins in close quarters and eventually ends up on the ground. I didn't quite know what he meant by that, but I was to soon find out.

After a while, Professor B stood up and Zhao quickly joined him, so I followed suit. "Are you ready for this Haley?" Professor B asked looking down at me.

"I think so Sir," I smiled uneasily.

"Relax," he assured me. "I want you to enjoy yourself and feel free to ask as many questions as you want. If you find yourself in a bad position or you cannot breath, all you have to do is tap. Do you know what that means?"

"Yes Sir," I said, remembering the countless UFC matches I had seen, when Kass' boyfriend Kyle would force us to watch with him all those Saturday nights. I didn't want to be a wimp and tap out.

"And don't worry, there is no shame in tapping out," he said as if he could read my mind. "It's the smart thing to do to avoid serious injury. Submission, we will break down into two parts; chokes and joint locks. Chokes, no problem. If you don't tap you'll go unconscious," he teased. "Joint locks, if you don't tap, something is going to break or at a minimum sustain a serious injury."

I stared at Professor B wide eyed. I wasn't so sure about this.

"You'll be fine," Zhao said, leading me to the center of the mat.

The first position Professor B taught us was the mount position. He had me go on the bottom and then try to escape from Zhao who was on top. It took me several times, but pretty soon I was able to make some progress.

"Come on Claire!" Professor B cheered me on. "Remember, first secure the arm, second bend the knees, feet flat on the ground and next, step over his foot on the same side as the arm you have trapped."

I paid close attention to Professor B's instructions and

began to slowly back Zhao off.

Professor B continued to encourage me. "Okay Claire, now step three. Lift your hips and drive their weight and balance forward."

I did as he instructed, knocking Zhao off balance. "Good, now roll to your knees and place your hands on his biceps to protect your face."

One minute later, I had Zhao defeated and on his back, though secretly I'm sure he gave up a little too easily to encourage me. Professor B and I cheered my victory loudly while Zhao layed on the mats catching his breath.

Professor B looked down at me, "See? Easy right?"

"Yeah, easy for you," I smiled, catching my breath and wiping the sweat from my brow.

It was well past five when we took the shuttle back to the base. (The shuttle meaning another government van that picked us up.) Every muscle in my body ached, but somehow I felt so empowered. Just the few moves I learned today, made me feel like I could take on anyone.

That week I went to the Shack everyday. Professor B was the most amazing teacher I could have asked for. The man was unstoppable. He taught me defense and fighting techniques I had no idea I needed or could ever execute. He also taught me how to use my mind as well as my body to fight. Zhao was my opponent and was a difficult adversary at first, but by the end of the week, I started keeping up. My mind opened up to a whole different level of fighting. I could tell what Zhao's next move would be just by a quick breath he took or a slight move he made. Professor B nicknamed me "Ninja" for my quiet, but powerful moves on the mat and that was a title I carried with pride.

July was a hot and sticky month in Hawaii. I stayed busy learning from Professor B. Three days of my week was spent at the shack with him and Zhao, where I was slowly becoming a skilled fighter. Professor B was such a great teacher, that by the end of the month, I knew I could handle myself if need be.

Fridays I was usually at the hospital with Major Wang, where my day consisted of regular check ups, blood draws, heart monitoring, and anything else you could possibly think of. Despite how much I had grown accustomed to the blood draws, my heart still skipped a beat when I watched the pink tinted blood being drawn through the line and into the vile. Major Wang always graciously ignored the fact that my blood type didn't exist before me, but still I could see his mystified eyes through his composure. I noticed my records were taken by him, put into my folder and carried with him directly out of the room. I never saw nurses or any other medical personnel. Just Major Wang. I was pretty sure he was ordered to just do his job without any questions.

Anyways, my weekends were spent pretty much alone. (I had asked Zhao once if he wanted to hang out, but he mumbled something about gaming and I didn't want to be a bother.) I didn't mind at all though. Alone time meant flying time and I had flown out to my island the last couple of weekends and walked the desolate beaches in the middle of the night.

The last Friday night in July, I found myself alone in my room again. I hadn't heard from Johnny in two and a half weeks and even then, that was just a short texting session. I didn't have a clue where he was or if he had even left the states yet.

I lay on my bed, watching the ceiling fan spin overhead, listening to some of the guys outside laughing and mingling around the barracks. I didn't dare try to join them. You had to be an elitist to fit in this group and despite their kind tolerance of me, I was welcome to kindly sit on the outside and watch, but never join in. It was made known to me that I was the first female to ever be in this unit and I had to earn my way into their confidence.

The sun disappeared over the horizon as the stars began popping through the brilliant purple and navy sky. What a perfect night for flying. I thought about my island and how much I would love to be there, especially in the daytime. There was so much exploring I wanted to do that couldn't be done at night.

That's when I got an idea. A crazy idea that my mom would probably freak out on if she knew.

I grabbed my backpack and went into my kitchenette. I filled it with bottles of water, snacks, fruit, my favorite book, my bikini, a couple of towels, and anything else I thought I would need on a deserted island. Tomorrow morning, well before the sun rose, I would be flying there to spend the day.

TWENTY-TWO

FOUR A.M. CAME very early the next day. My alarm sounded and despite only getting 4 hours of sleep, I immediately got up in anticipation of my day on the island.

I slipped a sweatshirt over a soft tee, my bikini, and some denim shorts, then slid on my white chucks. I threw my long spiral curls into a high bun and didn't even worry about makeup. I would be completely and totally alone and I couldn't wait.

My phone flashed fully charged at 4:10 am. I did a final check of my room as I slipped my arms into the straps of my backpack and tightened it as much as possible.

The slider door creaked in the silence of the morning as I stepped out onto my small balcony. The air was thick and dewy and I could tell it was going to be a hot Saturday. I stood and listened for a moment before flying up to the roof of the building, then checked each side to make sure no one was around. The streets below were empty and quiet without a soul in sight. When I felt it was safe enough, I launched myself straight up into the sky. The higher I got, the more likely I was to not be seen. I learned quickly in high school that flying straight up was much safer than across. Once I reached my cruising altitude, I would then begin to fly to my destination. At 500 feet I felt safe enough and shot across the starry sky above the black ocean below.

The sun was just about to peek over the east Pacific waters, when I arrived. I hovered in the air for a moment, scanning the entire island for any movement, before landing on the south beach.

I set my backpack safely on a large flat rock that protruded out of the sand, making a natural table top to sit on. I spread out my small blanket and took off my sweatshirt, using it as a pillowcase on my backpack, then propped myself against it to watch the sun rise. Bobby Darin's "Beyond the Sea" flowed from my playlist, as the sun rose its majestic face above the waters of the Pacific. A fiery orange and yellow glow spread across the waves and warmed my face as I rested from my flight. Before I knew it, I dozed off listening to the waves slide up the sand around me and fell into the most restful sleep I had in weeks.

A seagull called down at me, as a spray of ocean water mist cooled my skin. I opened my eyes to the sun shining directly above, in the clear blue sky. I sat slowly up and felt a familiar ache on my arms. My bright pink forearms were a contrast to the pale skin under my tee. Darn it! Sunburn again. I should have put my sunblock on first thing. I grabbed it out of my backpack and rubbed in a generous helping all over my body.

With the sun being almost directly above me in the sky, I assumed it had to be at least noon. I was close. It was already 11:20! I scolded myself for having slept the morning away, but at least I still had the whole day here. I couldn't fly out until it was completely dark anyway.

I grabbed a bottle of water and my phone and decided to do a little exploring through the tropical woods. I could have flown above it, but didn't want to miss the beauty and sounds of the island at ground level.

I ducked into a small opening in the trees. A natural path wound through the large plants and tropical flowers that popped in vivid colors against the brilliant greenery. I gasped at the beauty that surrounded me and stopped to smell every exotic flower possible. This was so unreal. No trace of human life or occupancy was anywhere to be found, not even animals, except for some of the most colorful birds I had ever seen. They stared down at me, looking somewhat puzzled to see me there.

A couple of times the brush was a little too thick and I had to fly over, but for the most part I was able to walk. Within no time, I had made it to the other side of the island. The north side was completely different from the south. There were no beaches here, just tall rocky cliffs that rose out of the ocean. I flew up to the highest one, that stood three stories above the surface of the ocean. The rocky wall extended the whole length of the east side, but to the west a small beach started after the rock ended and wrapped the rest of the way around.

I popped into the sky about 50 feet, just to get a better view and see what was around. For miles and miles, nothing but blue water stretched out before me. Not even a boat was in sight. This little island was perfect. Enough room to explore, but small enough to not get lost.

I jumped off the cliff and flew down to where the beach began and decided to follow it around to the south side. The waves crashed against the rock wall and slid sideways around and up to the beach, where I found a rock to sit on and take my shoes off. My toes slid into the powdery white sand and I sat for a moment to enjoy the cool spray on my sunburn. A breeze topped it off and the burn melted away.

Suddenly, a hollow sound echoed from behind and I jumped in the air in defense mode. I turned to find nothing behind me and followed the noise to a large opening in the rock wall. Had I not been in the air, I would have completely missed it. I flew closer to the cave and looked inside, careful to keep my distance. A light beamed down from an opening in the top towards the back of the cave, revealing a large room about the size of my apartment. When I felt it was safe, I went in and looked around. No bats, no vampires, nobody, just a cave with smooth rock walls and plenty of light inside. It was much too high for the water to reach, making the powdery white sand floor dry and warm on my feet. My mind began to race. This cave had a lot of potential and would be the perfect place to store my stuff, if need be, as I planned on spending a lot of time on this little island.

I jumped out of the cave and onto the beach below. The walk around to the south side of the island was beautiful. Clear blue waves slid up the beach and back down again, covering my feet in warmth as the sand slid from underneath.

I spent the day swimming in the ocean, reading, snacking, collecting shells, and walking the beach, then sat on the west side of the island to watch the sunset that was even more stunning than the sunrise. Before I knew it, the day was over and I packed up my backpack to head to base.

"I am so back here next weekend," I said to a crab that scuttled across the sand. I laid back on the rock and when the last glimmer of light slipped behind the water, shot into the dark night.

TWENTY-THREE

"OOO, WHERE DID you get that terrible sunburn?" Zhao asked as we walked to the shack that Tuesday.

"Oh, I fell asleep in the sun," I shrugged.

"Are you going to be able to roll with that?" he asked lightly, touching my arms.

"I can still kick your tushy," I laughed.

"We'll see about that," he smiled, pushing his glasses up his nose. "Honestly though Claire, you have really come a long way in these few weeks. Professor Corral even thinks so."

"Thanks Zhao," I smiled genuinely, as he opened the door for me. "You and Professor B are like these Jiu Jitsu warriors straight out of an action movie. I will never be as great as that, but at least I feel confident that I can defend myself if need be."

Zhao nodded at me, "And that's what matters most."

So I was wrong about the *sun burn not hurting when I was rollin'* part. It did hurt. The mats in the shack are not the smoothest and they made rolling a little rough, but I had my gi on and it was a long sleeve, so that helped a lot.

A new airman joined us for training that day and I'm proud to say I took him down pretty easily. In his defense, this was all new to him, but he was over twice my size and I could tell it was a bit intimidating for him to be taken down by a girl. Guys never want to lose to a woman and this always escalates into a harder fight and I'm clearly at a disadvantage because of my size and strength.I'm sure he was wondering what in the heck I was doing in his Special Operations Unit. He looked every bit the part of an Air Force special forces candidate, while Zhao and especially me, looked like we could be David to his Goliath.

I was still pretty curious about Zhao and how he ended up here. I had created in my mind this facade of who he really was while hanging out on the island. My imagination included a mad scientist, an aerodynamic professor, or maybe he possessed some kind of super power like myself. At any rate, he was here with Professor Corral for a reason, just like me, and that reason involved something that pertained to keeping us safe and able to fight for ourselves.

At the end of the day, as I packed my belongings to head back to the base, Professor B came and sat beside me.

"How are you feeling about everything Claire?" he asked.

"Well, I know I have a long way to go, but I'm definitely feeling more confident in myself. I mean, I know if I'm in a bad situation I can put up a good fight."

"Well, you have come a long way this past month. I'm going to be meeting with the Lt. General at the end of the week and discuss your progress. I have a feeling he's going to be ok with moving you to the next phase of your training."

"Phase?' I asked. "What do you mean?"

Professor B shrugged his shoulders. "I'm not sure exactly. They haven't been forthcoming with information about you. Normally, I'll get a whole folder on an airman, but with you...nothing."

I bit my lip and twisted the bottom of my shirt in my awkwardness. "That…that is strange," I said quietly. "So, you're from Indiana?" I asked, trying to change the subject.

"Yes, Indiana. If you ever find yourself in the Midwest, I would like to introduce you to my wife Brianne. She's a Brazilian Jiu Jitsu World Champion and you are a warrior on the battlefield. You would make excellent training partners."

"I would love that, Professor B," I smiled at him.

A horn blared from outside.

"Claire, let's go!" called Zhao from across the room.

I turned again to Professor B. "Thank you Professor B. You are an amazing teacher and I'm so blessed to be training under you."

"You're welcome Claire," he said as we stood up and I grabbed my bag. Professor B placed his hand gently on my pink arm. "You know Claire, I always push defensive mode, but if you ever find yourself in an overwhelming situation, remember it doesn't make one a coward to tap out....or run."

I nodded and smiled in genuine appreciation for his help and advice. Professor B had so many characteristics of my dad. Of course, my dad was not a skilled fighter like him, but he was always giving me the quirky, but wise advice Professor B did.

Professor B's last words hung heavy in my heart. I think deep inside he had a feeling about me. He knew my situation was an unusual one and he knew me getting into a bad situation was very possible. I wished so much I could tell him. I'm sure if he knew I could fly, he would be training me much differently.

I made up my mind to bring it up at the next meeting with Lt. General Gray.

Friday morning I arrived at Lt. General Gray's office early in anticipation of speaking to him before Captain Crew, Sgt. Mancuso, Major Wang, and Professor

Corral arrived. I entered the building just as Lt. General arrived and noticed he was somewhat startled to see me.

"Come on in, Haley," he said as I followed him into his office. "What are you doing here? Our meeting doesn't start for another 30 minutes."

"I'm sorry Sir," I apologized, "but I need to talk to you about something before Professor Corral gets here."

His eyebrows furrowed in concern.

"Nothing bad," I assured him.

He motioned to the chair across from his desk. "Have a seat."

I sat down and cleared my throat. "Well, first I want to thank you for giving me jiu jitsu classes with Professor Corral. He's been amazing and I've learned so much from him."

"He did say you've picked it up really fast," Lt. General smiled.

I blushed at his compliment. "I feel pretty good about it. A lot safer and surer of myself."

"Well, you certainly seem more confident. I could see it in your eyes when you walked in."

"I think I'm in the best shape I've ever been in, Lt. General. Rolling at the shack and those log hikes every morning are kicking my tail, but waking up some muscles I didn't even know I had."

"Yeah, they'll do that," he laughed at me. "So what's going on? What can I do for you?"

"Well, I was just wondering why Professor Corral

doesn't know about me yet. I mean, I think that would change a lot about the way he's training me if he knew. I could learn some techniques from the air."

Lt. General glared at me for a moment, rubbing his chin in thought before he finally spoke. "Airman Haley, I understand your thought process with all this...and I'm sure it would make a difference in the way you are trained, but the top brass has made the decision that very few people are to know about you. Enough people know already and if someone does leak you to the public, we are still able to control the situation without it getting out of hand. The more people who know, the more difficult it will be to contain it, and the more evidence they will have against us...against you." He stood up and walked around to the front of his desk and leaned on it folding his arms. "Right now, you're just a myth, like an alien or vampires. We can deny it and explain you away, but the more people who know, the more difficult that becomes. Understand?"

I nodded my head. I knew that was what he was going to say, but it was worth a try anyway.

"Can I ask you another question?"

"Sure."

"Zhao. What's his story?"

He smiled, shaking his head at me. "I knew this was coming. Zhao...Zhao is an aeronautical engineer. In fact, as of right now, he is the smartest one in the country... umm, very astounding for his young age. We basically brought him here to see if he can figure you out."

"But he doesn't even know about me."

"Well, not yet. He will know, but for right now, we need to know that we can trust him. That's why he's in your unit. If he can stick it out and adjust to this team, that speaks volumes about him."

"And so far?" I asked.

"He's one of the hardest working airmen there. I think he's going to fit into our little secret just fine."

I nodded and smiled.

"Anything else?" he asked standing up.

"No Sir, that's all."

"Ok, I'm going to bring the gentlemen in. It's about that time."

Soon, Wang, Mancuso, Professor Corral and Crew joined us in the office. Capt. Crew frowned at me, surprised that I was already there. I didn't understand why he disliked me so much.

We discussed my progress and the next phase of training. I would be headed to an airfield called Dillingham that sat directly on the coast, starting next Monday. The only catch is that all my training would be done at night. I was to report to my unit every morning for PT, break until 3pm, and then report to the airfield. Fridays I would still be training with Professor B and Zhao.

Captain Crew and the rest of the men were puzzled.

"So she's doing night training?" Captain Crew pressed.

"That's when we can get the proper people there," Lt. General vaguely explained.

Captain Crew leaned up in his seat. "Sir, I don't

understand…" he began, but Lt. General cut him off with a short, "Orders from the top." Captain Crew frowned at being denied information on my case again and shot me another irritated glance. But that was that. He asked no more questions and I breathed a silent sigh of relief.

Of course I knew why I would be there at night. I could do test flights over the ocean, undetected in the darkness and I couldn't wait!

Lt. General dismissed the gentlemen and I waited to speak to him once more.

"I tell you Claire, it's not easy to keep this quiet. I don't like keeping secrets from my men and they don't like being out of the loop."

"I definitely can tell that with Captain Crew," I said curtly, but then immediately regretted my starchiness.

Lt. General glared at me, then his eyes softened. "Claire, cut Captain Crew a break. He knows something's up and I can imagine how difficult it is for a man of his rank to not know or understand what is going on and … and on a personal level," he lowered his voice, "Captain Crew has been through a lot this past year. He almost lost his teenage daughter to a drug overdose this spring. He's…he's been through a lot."

I gasped slightly and hung my head, immediately regretting every bad thought I ever had about Captain Crew. My mom's voice popped into my head. *"Always be kind Claire. You never know what someone is going through."*

"Now, that's just between us. Not many people know about it."

"I'm sorry, Sir." I apologized to Lt. General. "I'll try to move past it."

I made up my mind right then to be as nice as I could be to Captain Crew and maybe even try to befriend him. That would definitely make my mom proud.

TWENTY-FOUR

AT 4 A.M. sharp Saturday morning, Michael Buble's "Fly Me To The Moon" streamed from my phone to wake me. I rolled over in my bed, the day before me, looming ahead. First formation, PT, breakfast, and then meet with Zhao to catch the shuttle...*"Fly me to the moon, let me play among the stars and let me see what spring is like on Jupiter and Mars..."* Michael Buble's smooth voice filled my ears. I rolled over again to look at my phone. 4:04 am. Wait a second. Today was Saturday! Saturday, as in Island Day! Beach Day! Nap Day! Exploring Day! I was going back to spend the whole day at my island! Claire's Island!

I jumped from the bed immediately and grabbed my clothes. I had everything packed and ready to go. This time I was bringing a small portable hammock I had found at Walmart this week. I also packed plenty of sunblock, sandwiches (because the snacks didn't pack enough energy for me last weekend), water, binoculars, and my latest read. I brushed my teeth and then slipped my gray tee shirt dress over my bikini and grabbed my very heavy backpack. You would think I was going to camp out for a whole weekend with how full it was.

I did my normal routine of flying to the roof, scoping out the area, and finally shooting straight into the dark, early morning sky. I don't know if you've ever seen the stars just before sunrise, but they are so bright, and for some reason this time of morning is when I see shooting stars the most. Today was no exception. With the black ocean below me and the dark sky above, I looked up at one of the most incredible meteor showers I had ever seen. They crisscrossed overhead leaving a stream of bright orange gases and fire behind them. I gasped at their beauty, almost scared at one point that I would collide with one of them. There were too many to count. I pulled my phone from my pocket and began recording for Kass. She would really get a kick out of this.

A half hour later, I touched down on my island. I landed on my usual rock slab and waited for the sun to start rising. This sunrise was just as stunning as last week. I grabbed my phone and snapped pics and videos to send to Kass tonight.

She was calling me to "talk about something really important" so I had to be back on time to get her call. My service dropped like a hot cake all the way out here.

When the sun was full in the pristine blue sky, I layed back on my towel and backpack to rest for a few. My eyes were beginning to get heavy, when the sound of water splashing caught my attention. I sat straight up. In the distance a gray object surfaced from the water and immediately went back under. I grabbed the binoculars and spotted a pod of dolphins swimming off the south shore. I shed my shoes and my gray tee dress, grabbed my goggles, and popped into the sky above the tall, swaying palm trees.

Out in the ocean the dolphins jumped in the air playing, clicking and whistling at each other. I had never been close to a dolphin before and my curiosity went into overdrive. I flew higher into the air and scanned the ocean all around for any signs of human eyes. All clear!

Out closer to the dolphins, I hovered above the surface of the water before diving in. I swam close to the splashing and chattering and before I knew it, was in a swarm of fins and splashing water. My heart raced, as their rubbery bodies brushed up against my skin. Dolphins don't bite, do they?

I slid on my oversized goggles and dove under water. The bright sun shot sunbeams into the clear water, as the dolphins swam in and out of the light, circling around me, curious as to what I was doing there with them. I resurfaced and took a deep breath, then immediately went under again. The dolphins dove into the sky and back into the water so gracefully, leaving thousands of white bubbles floating to the surface.

"They're beautiful," I thought to myself underwater.

I resurfaced again and took a deep breath, making a mental note to bring snorkeling equipment with me the next trip out.

Water rippled behind me and I turned, startled to find myself face to face with a large dolphin. She had the biggest smile on her face, revealing four rows of shiny white teeth.

"Hi there," I said to her. "I bet you're wondering what I'm doing here, huh girl?"

She nodded her head back and forth and I giggled at her, slowly holding out my hand to pet her rubbery cheek. She seemed to appreciate that and then sank into the water closer to me.

"Awe, you're so cute!" I said as she snuggled my arm. What an amazing miracle this critter was. God was so creative.

A brisk breeze pushed a wave over my shoulder and a loud clap to the west of us caught my attention. I looked at the sky that had suddenly turned a green/gray color. Large dark clouds rolled toward us and my new friend quickly disappeared under the waves. I took that as a sign to get out of there too.

I flew out of the water and back to my rock slab. The wind whistled loudly through the palm trees, blowing my hair and sending a chill through my body, despite the 84 degree temperature. Maybe I should have checked the weather forecast for the day.

My mind raced trying to figure out where I was going

to take cover in all of this. I couldn't fly back, because despite the darkness of the storm I would still be seen. I dried off quickly and threw on my tee shirt dress and sweat pants I bought for the trip home.

Light speckles of rain fell softly against my cheek, as I looked for some kind of shelter. Then I remembered. The cave! I snatched up my belongings and headed to the north side of the island. The palm trees leaned to the east beneath me as a strong westerly wind pushed into the island, making flying a little difficult. I landed safely in front of the cave entrance and found my way inside just in time. Thunder roared and lightning clapped outside, but in the cave I stayed dry and warm, the heat of the day still locked inside. I pulled out my hammock bed and laid it on the soft sand. Light and a little rain streamed in from the hole in the top back of the cave, but I took out my large flashlight to help me see a little better. Hawaiian tropical storms seemed to blow over fast, so hopefully this one wouldn't take too long.

I unpacked my lunch and ate, then cozied up with my large towel to do a little reading. The last chapter I remember reading was 12, before my eyes grew heavy and I fell into a long afternoon nap.

TWENTY-FIVE

"I GOT IT!" I heard a voice echo around me as I rolled to my back on the hammock. My eyes slowly opened to the sound of waves crashing and rain still lightly falling outside. I rubbed my eyes to adjust them to the scarce light and looked around trying to figure out where I was. *That's right. The storm. The cave. Wait, did I just hear...*

"I said I got it!" I heard the voice yell louder.

I shot up from my hammock bed and looked toward the entrance of the cave, catching my breath as my heart beat loudly in my chest. I scurried to the entrance and peeked out below. A small boat was docked on the beach, with four men busily working to unload white packages from it onto the sand. In the distance, not too far off shore, a large yacht sat anchored in place, a bright emerald green stripe down the side of it flashing against the water, as it rolled up and down on the waves.

A dog barking caught my attention and I glanced back down at the men on the beach. A large German Shepherd frantically paced back and forth at the bottom of the rocks that led up to the cave, his bark becoming more anxious as he looked up and we locked eyes.

"Shut your dog up, Lewis!" the big guy with a long beard yelled.

"Something's up there," Lewis yelled back, walking towards the dog.

"Phantom! Come here, boy!"

All the men stopped and looked in my direction, and I ducked behind the rock at the entrance of the cave.

"Well, get up there and check it out!" the bearded man yelled.

I ran in and gathered my stuff. It would take them a good few minutes to get up the rocks, but I threw everything in as quickly as I could. Phantom's ferocious bark got closer and closer as I struggled to grab it all. If I left anything, they would know I was there and that would be a really bad thing. Really bad, because I was no dummy. I knew what was in those packages. Drugs. Enough drugs that they would not want anyone to have witnessed them bringing it to this island.

I zipped my backpack and grabbed the hammock. Not enough time to pack it in with everything else. I ran to the back of the cave where the light was coming through and rain was trickling in. I would have to fly through the water and out of the hole in the top.

Phantom's bark echoed into the cave and within moments he came running toward me. I shot up through the hole just in time, as the rain soaked through my hair and clothes. The chilly water poured over me taking my breath away and I glanced down to see Phantom looking up at me, his teeth snarling, jumping in the air in a final attempt to reach me.

I climbed the rocks the rest of the way out of the cave and disappeared into the thick island brush. When I felt safe, I stopped to catch my breath by a tall palm tree. My hands were shaking as I cupped them to my mouth to try and calm my frantic breathing. I panicked knowing I was stuck on the island. I could possibly fly away if I had to, but there was too great a risk of being seen with all the military aircraft flying in the area and I didn't want to go to the other side of the island to hide. I had to keep these guys in sight. I wanted to know where they were and when they left.

I looked at the tall palm tree above me. That would be the perfect hiding place. I grabbed my phone, binoculars, and towel and hid my backpack and hammock in the thick brush not far away. I flew straight up the back of the palm tree and situated myself in the palm branches, that made a perfect umbrella sheltering me from the rain. Way down below, the men busily carried the white packages from the beach and into the cave. Lewis was doing his best to calm down Phantom, who was still barking and pacing back and forth looking for me. Fortunately, he had lost my scent in the cave when I flew out with all the rain coming in.

"Lewis, get over here!" the mean man yelled. "Leave that dog alone and help us! We have 20 minutes to get this load in!"

Lewis, who looked like he couldn't be any older than me, immediately went to help. I sat patiently in the palm tree, watching them through my binoculars and recording what I could with my phone, occasionally hearing what they were saying through the swishing of the rain through the palms.

I turned my focus to the yacht to see if I could see how many people were on board. Through the glass of the cockpit, I could make out two people, and on the side of the vessel, the name "Sydney Jo." Whoever owned that boat had a lot of money and it was pretty obvious how they got it.

The twenty minute timeline that they had given themselves turned into an hour and by the time everything was in the cave, the sun had come back out. My legs cramped as I stayed still, crumpled in a ball to fit in the palm branches.

Lewis grabbed Phantom and put him in the boat and the other men soon joined them. They puttered back to the yacht and boarded. Within minutes, the yacht sped off towards the east. I stayed in the tree until all I could see left of the yacht was a tiny speck on the blue water, then stretched out my legs and jumped down from the palm tree. I grabbed my stuff and flew down inside of the cave again. Stacked against the wall were packages upon packages of drugs. I wasn't too sure, but from what I had seen in my twenty short years, it was probably cocaine. (I remember seeing it packaged just like this in a video in high school.)

I stared at them, my arms folded, biting my lip in frustration. There was nothing I could do about it. This was a no win situation. I couldn't report it anywhere without someone knowing I had been here. On top of that, I felt like I lost my island. There was no way I could come back here, knowing this was a drug trafficking area. I would never feel safe.

I flew out of the cave and down to the white beach below where the men had just been, their footprints and paw prints still fresh in the sand. I took off my tee shirt dress, sweats, and shoes and started walking to the other side of the beach in my swimsuit, the sun beating down on me. I pulled my wet hair into a bun and let the waves splash over my feet. It was so beautiful here. I didn't want to give up my little island to a bunch of lame, drug traffickers.

The rest of the day slipped quickly away and occasionally I would pop into the sky to make sure the yacht or whoever was supposed to pick up the drugs wasn't coming around. I hated this. I felt so safe here. What a waste of a beautiful place.

The sun sank majestically into the sea, leaving an amazing burst of brilliant color across the western sky. I sat on my rock and stayed until the last possible moment I could. When the colors melted into a brilliant royal, then midnight blue, I grabbed my backpack from under the brush, strapped it on, then rocketed into the starry night sky.

What a day it had been. I was dirty and exhausted and just wanted to go to bed. Back at my apartment, I took a long hot shower and layed down, trying to let the stress of the day go, but it was well after two before I finally drifted off to sleep.

TWENTY-SIX

THE NEXT MORNING, my phone ringing in my ear at 7 am, woke me with a start. I looked at the number. It was Kass. I had forgotten to call her last night.

"Hello?" I muttered.

"Claire?"

Oh no. I could tell by her voice she was irritated. I rolled over in bed and leaned up. "Hey Kass," I said sweetly.

"Claire," she sighed, annoyed. "Do you know I waited up until midnight for your call? I tried calling you all day, but it just kept going to voicemail."

"I'm so sorry, Kass," I said through a yawn. "Phones are really tricky out here in the islands...plus, I didn't get home until late last night."

"Well... well I told you I had to talk to you. It's really

important."

The desperation in her voice was like a jolt, knocking the drowsiness right out of my body.

"What?! What is it?! Are you ok? Is mom, Darcy, and Tessa ok?!"

"Yes, yes! Everyone's ok, but I have some bad news for you."

I took a deep breath, my mind immediately going to Johnny in Afghanistan.

"J...Johnny?" I whispered.

"No! No, it's not Johnny!" she said emphatically. "Would you please listen! It's mom. Mom and Major Silva!"

I let out a sigh of relief and rolled my eyes in frustration. "Kass, what is it? Are you still thinking they like each other?"

"Oh Claire, I don't think. I KNOW!"

I rubbed my eyes, the lack of sleep and salt water yesterday, making them feel extra dry. "And how do you know this Kass?"

"Well, maybe because he's been coming over for Sunday lunch every week *and* going to church with mom *and* sitting with her. He finds every excuse to drop by and he takes her to lunch at least once a week while they're working! I mean it's worse than when you left!" Kass exclaimed, finally catching her breath.

"Well..." I said shrugging my shoulders.

"Well what?!" she asked.

"Well Kass...I mean what's wrong with that?"

Kass was silent for a moment and I could tell she was frustrated just by the way she was breathing.

"Kass…?"

"It's just that…she still loves dad, Claire. I know she does. I think she's just allowing him to come around because she misses you and he's keeping her updated on you."

"Wait. What do you mean keeping her updated on me?"

"You know, he lets her know what you're doing, your progress, your daily activities…"

That was interesting information to know. Someone was monitoring my every move and sending information back to Campbell. I wondered if they still had meetings about me.

"Kass," I said in the most calm voice I could. "Mom does still love dad. Mom will always love dad, but mom is also alone. I'm out here and you leave next year for college and where does that leave her? If she's going to be hanging out or dating a guy, I'm glad it's Sebastian. He is one of the nicest guys I have ever known."

I heard Kass sniffle through the phone. My heart broke that she was crying and I couldn't be there to wrap my arms around her.

"When are you coming home?" she asked, her voice cracking. "I miss you Claire. It's just not the same without you."

"Aww Kass," I said, "trust me, I want to come home. I don't think it's going to be much longer."

"But you're missing my whole senior year."

Oh wow. She might as well have punched me in the gut with that statement. I hated it so much that I wasn't in the house with her the final few months before she left for college.

I took a deep breath and pulled myself together. She didn't need to hear me in my weakness right now. She needed me in big sister mode. I did my best to try and reassure her. "I know and trust me, I'm going to have a conversation with Lt. General Gray about it. He seems like he cares about what's going on with me. I promise you, I'll be home by Christmas." I paused for a moment, speaking more softly to her. "But Kass, in the meantime, give Major Silva a break. I'm glad he's around and taking care of you and mom. I worry about you guys all the time."

Kass was quiet for a moment. "Ok," she finally agreed, blowing her nose loudly through the phone. She was so loud, I had to hold the phone away from my ear. "So what are they doing to you out there? Have you been able to fly?"

I spent the next hour on the phone with her, trying to cheer her up with all my stories of the Coast Guard arrest I saw, my favorite perch on the light house, Zhao, Professor Corral and jiu jitsu, and finally the island and my swim with the dolphins. Of course, I left off the part about the drug pirates.

Kass was enthralled with the island part and I promised to send her videos. When I felt like she was in a better mood, we hung up. I found the video I took of my island adventures and the meteor shower I had seen and sent it to her right away. I felt so bad for her, but also felt good knowing Major Silva was hanging around them like he had promised he would.

I layed back down and watched in awe, of a couple of the videos I had taken. I still couldn't believe what an incredible life I had.

TWENTY-SEVEN

MONDAY EVENING A shuttle picked up Zhao and I. We were told to get a lot of sleep today, because we would be working late into the night. Everyone in our company was leaving the barracks and on their way to dinner, when we boarded the shuttle. They looked curiously, mumbling to themselves and shooting cold glances at us. I felt kind of guilty skipping out on PT and the daily activities, but at the same time I was excited for whatever was going to happen at the airfield tonight.

"Do you think the guys are mad because we seem to be getting preferential treatment?" he asked, sliding his glasses back up his nose.

I looked at him a bit confused. "You mean because they skipped us out of PT today?"

"Yeah, that and we're pretty much never in training

with everyone else. What's the point of being in such an exclusive unit, but never doing the things they're doing? If we deploy somewhere, we're not going to have any inkling of what to do."

I shrugged my shoulders like I didn't know why, but truth be told, Zhao and I were only in that unit to keep us safe. Well, me safe. Poor Zhao just got caught up in my mess.

"I don't know Zhao," I said. "Maybe we can talk to Lt. General about it."

I looked out the window and watched the beach stream past us, the palm trees and businesses flying by in the late evening sunset. Ooooo...there's Taco Bell! Focus Claire. What could I possibly do tonight at the airfield without Zhao knowing I could fly? Lt. General said they had plans on telling Zhao and I wondered if tonight would be the night.

We pulled into Dillingham Airfield 20 minutes later. I gasped at the view of the ocean from the airstrip.

"Haley! Zhao!" I looked over at a large hangar building, where Lt. General had the door opened for us. "Come on over!"

Zhao and I walked toward the building where Lt. General led us inside and down a hall to a lounge area that looked like a small cafeteria. On the table were sub sandwiches, chips, and drinks.

"Have you guys eaten?" he asked.

"No Sir," we answered in unison. I was so nervous and excited about tonight, I hadn't even thought to eat.

"Well, go ahead and help yourself. The others will be here soon."

"Thank you, Sir," we both said together again.

He left the room and Zhao and I went to the table to get food.

"Others?" Zhao whispered as he spread mustard on his sandwich. "What's going on Claire?"

I shrugged my shoulders again. "It's ok, Zhao. I'm sure they'll explain everything."

We sat down at the table and ate. I tried to talk about jiu jitsu to keep his mind occupied, but everytime we heard a noise outside the lounge, Zhao would almost jump and look around, as if he were nervous about something. Maybe telling him wasn't such a great idea. I didn't know if he could handle it or not.

To my surprise, Command Sergeant Major Williams, who had been at the meeting at Ft. Campbell before I left, walked in. I must have looked startled to see him because he mouthed "surprise" to me and Zhao stared at me suspiciously. Didn't he work at the Pentagon? What was he doing all the way out here?

Another man, who could have been an exact replica of Zhao, only older, followed him.

Zhao's eyes grew wide, then he jumped from his seat. "Dad!" he exclaimed, while my mouth popped open in surprise.

"Hey son!" his dad exclaimed while Zhao jumped into his open arms and they hugged for a long moment. My eyes misted over with tears for Zhao. It was obvious they hadn't seen each other in a long while.

After introductions all around they joined us in eating. Dr. Zhao was an impressive man to say the least. It was very intimidating just sitting in his presence and hearing of his work with NASA in Houston and I could tell Command Sergeant Major Williams felt the same.

Now Zhao was more than eager to share his knowledge of flight with us also.

Even though I didn't understand half the things he was saying, I was so impressed with his background in aeronautics. I knew Zhao was a smart guy, but even more than that was how brilliant he was. No wonder why they hooked him up with me. Maybe between him and his dad, they could figure out how my body was doing this and more importantly how to keep me from losing my power to fly.

I excused myself to the bathroom as everyone was finishing up dinner. When I came out, Lt. General Gray was waiting for me in the hallway.

"Claire, I just thought I would let you know, we are going to be telling the Zhaos tonight," he said in a hushed voice. "If it's ok with you, I thought you could get the ball rolling by just telling them what happened to you and then I'll take over."

I swallowed hard. I shouldn't have been so nervous since I had told this so many times, but I was.

"You don't have to if you don't want to," he reassured me when I broke out in my nervous red blotches. "I can do it, but I thought it would be easier for him and his dad both if they heard the story from the beginning. You know, so we don't just throw it on them."

"Oh no, it's fine," I said, nodding in agreement. "I can do it." I didn't mean to be such a wimp.

I followed him back into the lounge, where he shut the door behind us. I stood at the end of the table and they stopped midconversation to look at me and Lt. General. Thankfully Lt. General got the ball rolling.

"So first of all I want to thank you guys for coming, especially you Dr. Zhao, flying all the way here from Houston." He then turned to Zhao, "So Airman Zhao, you've been here for four months now. I know we've been having you do some odd experiments and stretching your brain a bit, but there has been a reason for all of this." He turned and nodded in my direction. "Airman Haley is obviously a big part of it and I'll let her tell you her story. Let me remind you that what you hear today is a top governmental secret and I actually have some forms that I need you both to sign for your commitment to secrecy. If you wish to opt out of this, we can dismiss you both and you are free to go...but we are requesting that you help us with your knowledge and expertise in aeronautics, not only for the benefit of our country, but for the safety of Claire."

Zhao looked at me with concern in his eyes, then at LT. General Gray. "Give me the papers. I'd do anything to protect Claire."

Again my eyes misted over and I smiled at him. "Thank you, Zhao," I said quietly.

Dr. Zhao motioned for the pen across the table. "Of course," he smiled at me too.

They signed the paperwork and then the floor was mine. I took a deep breath. "Well, here it goes," I smiled nervously. "In the summer of 2017, I was getting ready to start my senior year. I met my boyfriend Johnny, who was a soldier and an aspiring helicopter pilot in the Army, stationed at Ft. Campbell. One night while I was hanging out with him in the airfield hangar as he was pulling guard duty, I had an accident with what I found out later, was a failed WWII military experiment. I got a cut on my arm and the next day, the cut was gone and this tattoo was in its place." I held my wrist to show the gentlemen my Saturn rings.

I watched as Dr. Zhao's mouth dropped open, his eyes wide in shock. I quickly tucked my hands back into my pant's pocket, a little embarrassed and continued on.

"So the next night I went out for a jog ...and...and I realized I was being followed by these two bad men. When I went to run away from them, I started..." I stopped suddenly. It felt like there was a big cotton ball stuck in my throat. I nervously twisted the bottom of my shirt, took a deep breath and swallowed hard, collecting my thoughts. Their eyes bore into me, as they sat on the edge of their seats waiting to hear the rest. I looked at Lt. General Gray who smiled slightly at me, nodding his head, silently encouraging me to continue.

"Well...I... I started flying."

Zhao and his father looked at me like they didn't hear

me at first and then a second time like I was crazy.

"What?" Zhao asked in disbelief. "What are you talking about, Claire?"

"I can fly, Zhao. Umm...you know, like Superman. I can fly like Superman."

Zhao shook his head in denial at me, while Dr. Zhao sat staring off past me not in disbelief, but in deep thought. I looked at Lt. General Gray who kindly stepped in to help me out.

"It's true Gentlemen. I'm sorry. I know it's hard to believe, but we've seen it for ourselves," he said nodding at Command Sergeant Major Williams.

"How can it be possible?" Dr. Zhao asked, almost to himself. "I mean, we thought that it could, maybe someday…"

Maybe if I gave them all the background information that I had on it that would help. I began explaining all I found out about Major Kearney and all I knew about his involvement in creating the pink potion. Dr. Zhao perked up as soon as I mentioned the name Kearney.

"Kearney? Major Brian Kearney?"

"Yes…" I said surprised he knew of Major Kearney. "Did you know him?"

"Yes! I worked with him and his dad was my mentor in Houston for years."

I gasped, surprised to meet anyone with any ties to the Kearneys at all. I couldn't believe what I was hearing.

Lt. General opened the floor for questioning and we sat for an hour discussing it all. Dr. Zhao and I shot questions back and forth at each other, him asking me all about how my body worked with flying and me questioning him about the Kearneys, and his role in their experiments.

When we were done, Lt. General escorted us to the hangar outside, where I demonstrated my flying capabilities to them all. That was an interesting 30 minutes. Zhao paced back and forth with his hands planted firmly on the back of his head, continuously repeating "I can't even believe this right now," and "Oh my god! Is this even real?" Meanwhile, Dr. Zhao kept coming over and checking me out in between flights and he was particularly interested in my tattoo.

"I remember this," he said. "Brian had this same tattoo. We all teased him about it." He then looked at me with concern. "Claire, you do know he died, right?"

I nodded my head yes.

"Wait a minute," he paused, a light bulb going off in his head… "He died from unknown traumatic injuries. Did he?"

"He fell out of the sky," I answered nodding my head.

"Claire!" Zhao exclaimed, listening in from his pacing. "Are you serious?"

"Airman Zhao, we're not going to let that happen to Claire," Command Sergeant Major Williams said. "She is under a strict 'no fly' rule, right Claire?"

"Yes Sir," I said, inwardly cringing, because I knew that wasn't happening.

It was after ten when we finally left. It was decided that

Dr. Zhao would be staying for the next two weeks and we would be spending every day at the airfield. Poor Zhao and his dad. We finally got Zhao calmed down, but they both left the airfield looking like they had seen a ghost.

I came home that night feeling emotionally drained, but relieved that Zhao knew, and he and his father were both on board now. They were so smart, I was sure they would be able to figure me out.

I checked my phone before I fell asleep, in hopes of hearing something from Johnny. It had been over a month since his last text and even with everything going on in my life, there was a constant worry about him in the back of my mind.

TWENTY-EIGHT

I SPENT THE week at the airfield. Each night we would start off with me flying in the hangar (under tight security outside) and then moving to the beach after midnight when Lt. General thought everything was clear. It was pretty much a lot of what I did in Houston, except I got to fly out over the ocean. They had given me this black body suit that had a GPS locator on it and also a parachute strapped to my back for extra safety. The GPS must have worked well, because Zhao said within seconds of me taking off, they lost visual and only knew where I was because of the GPS.

On Thursday night, Lt. General Gray approached Zhao, his dad, and myself.

"Do you guys have any plans this weekend?" he asked.

"Well, I'm flying home for the weekend," Dr. Zhao

answered, "but I'll be back on Monday."

"I have nothing going on," Zhao shrugged, then they all looked at me.

I did have plans that I was very much looking forward to and that was going to my island. After last weekend, I thought I would never go back again, but I just couldn't stay away. Besides that, I was just a little too stubborn to let some drug dealers ruin it for me.

"Well, nothing concrete," I answered.

"Good," Lt. General said. "This Saturday night is the Officer's Ball and the higher ups are requesting you both there."

Zhao and I looked at each other in bewilderment. "Us?" I almost laughed. "Why us?"

"Because it was requested," Lt. General said with a mischievous smile.

"Well….I guess we're going to a ball," Zhao laughed.

"Wait a second. Zhao and I have nothing to wear," I reasoned.

"Zhao will wear his dress uniform and Claire, there is a recycled dress shop downtown. Captain Crew's daughters utilize it all the time. They said you can find a dress there."

Recycled Dress shop. I imagined tons of sequins, ruffled collars, and large bows edging the bottom of poofy 80's prom gowns.

"Ok," I replied, trying to sound excited about the ball, but dreading it already.

Lt. General handed me a slip of paper with an address

scribbled on it.

"Take tomorrow off," Lt. General commanded us. "That way you'll have time to find a dress and the Zhaos can have some tourist time together."

We thanked him and grabbed our stuff to head back to base.

"Oh, Lt. General," I said as he scooped up his car keys and headed toward the door. "Is Sgt. Mancuso taking me?"

He paused for a moment. "No, he can't. I guess you can go alone, but you are to check in with Sgt. Mancuso before you go, and then again when you return. You have two hours to get there, get a dress, and head back, understand?"

"Yes Sir," I replied, excited that I would get to leave the base on my own.

"You can't leave base on your own?" Zhao asked as we climbed into his dad's rental.

"No," I said rolling my eyes.

"Why not?"

"I don't know. Something about spies or whatever," I said nonchalantly.

"Claire!" Zhao said, spinning around from the front seat, while his dad's eyes stared at me in shock from the rearview mirror.

"Zhao, it's fine," I yawned. I was way too tired for any drama.

"That's it. Dad and I are taking you to get a dress tomorrow."

"Oh, no you're not!" I laughed. "Zhao, I'm fine! Seriously, I want to go alone."

"But Claire…"

"No Zhao!" I said emphatically. "Thank you, but no."

Zhao turned around and slumped in his seat. He knew better than to argue with me.

The next morning I caught a cab into the city to find the dress shop. What I thought was going to be a boring time was actually a great one! I looked through the dresses and 30 minutes in, had already picked out 6 to try on. No sequins and bows here. I finally settled on an elegant form fitting navy blue one, that hung off my shoulders and lightly flared at the bottom. I could definitely tell this dress was vintage, and I'm not talking 80's vintage, but more like 60's vintage. I felt completely elegant and girly and I loved it. It had been so long since I had even put on a dress.

"Do you have shoes?" The sales lady asked.

"No Ma'am," I said, a little embarrassed. "I have nothing, actually. I just found out I was going to the ball yesterday and it's tomorrow night."

"Oh wow! Well, we can take care of that."

The sales lady, Kaena, was so helpful and friendly. We talked about my career in the Air Force and how she had grown up on the island. Her grandmother opened this shop in the 50's and had passed it on to her. On the wall were pictures of her and her family from each decade. What a wonderful family history.

"So how did you hear about my little shop?" she asked as we browsed the jewelry case.

"My Captain passed on the information to me. I guess his daughters come here," I explained, picking up a ruby red and diamond pair of teardrop earrings. These would match perfectly.

"What's his name?"

"Captain Crew," I answered.

I watched the smile on Kaena's face fade. "Oh," she simply said.

"Do you know them?" I asked curiously.

"Yes," she said smiling politely. "Let's just say they are very demanding."

I raised my eyebrows and gave her the "yikes" look, but wasn't surprised at all. If they were anything like their dad, I could see that happening for sure. "I'm sorry. I haven't met them yet."

"Have you ever seen Cinderella?" she asked.

"Oh, yes!" I laughed, knowing where she was going with that.

"The evil step sisters take two, for sure. They were here last weekend and it was all I could do to make them happy."

"Well, the apple doesn't fall from the tree," I smirked. "It sounds like I will get to meet them tomorrow night."

"Good luck with that," she laughed.

I liked Kaena. She was the first girl friend I had made

in a long time.

I made my purchases with 30 minutes to spare. I had enough time to grab a sub and a cab and get back to the base.

Sgt. Mancuso stared at me curiously as I checked back in with him, the long white formal gown bag slung over my shoulder.

"How did you get roped into the ball?" he laughed.

"Lt. General," I sighed.

"Well, the food is good," he smirked. "The music, *not* so much."

"Thanks Sgt. Mancuso," I smiled.

"I'll see you there, Haley."

TWENTY-NINE

SATURDAY EVENING I stood back and looked at myself in the full length mirror. The navy blue dress fit so perfectly, outlining every curve of my body and flaring out slightly at the bottom. Not to brag, but those PT exercises had really paid off. I always did my best to stay in shape and take care of myself, but between jiu jitsu and the log hikes I was finding muscles I didn't know existed. I pumped my biceps in the mirror and felt to see how hard they were.

"Hmm...not bad, Claire," I said to myself.

Pounding on the door made me jump. I grabbed my ruby red earrings and went to answer it. I opened it to Zhao who stood extra tall in his dress uniform. He took a breath and held his hand over his heart.

"Wow Claire. You are so...so stunning."

I blushed and put my earrings in. "Thank you Zhao. You clean up pretty nice yourself."

"Thanks. Look at you all patriotic."

"What?" I asked, wrinkling my nose at him.

"Patriotic. Blue dress, red earrings. Are your shoes white?"

"No," I laughed, showing him my retro velvet navy blue heels. "They're blue too."

"Well, are you ready to do this?" he asked.

"Yes Sir, just give me one minute."

I invited him in and went to the mirror to pull one side of my long curls back with a sparkly hair clip.

"Ok," I said, taking a deep breath and grabbing my clutch. "Let's fly."

We walked downstairs and out into the evening sunshine. Several guys from our unit were outside playing catch or talking on the steps. We walked past them, where a couple whistled our way and one told me how nice I looked.

"Thanks Henry," I smiled.

Zhao opened the door of his dad's rental for me and then got in on the other side.

"Man Claire, aren't you offended by the whistles and what Henry said to you?" he asked starting the car.

I rolled my eyes at him. "Really Zhao? What kind of a pansy do you think I am? That was really sweet of them...and I don't get offended easily. Now if they had touched me, I would have had to bust out some jiu jitsu on them."

He laughed. "Wow. You're different from a lot of girls I went to school with."

"I guess I just feel bad for guys nowadays. God forbid they actually compliment a lady."

"Well, they don't know how you can fight on the mat or that you fly like Supergirl, but I do. So I'm not taking any chances and keeping my mouth shut."

"Whatever Zhao," I blushed.

"Seriously though, Claire. I still can't believe all this," he said, pulling out of the parking lot. "I wake up every morning thinking it's all a dream. I can't even wrap my mind around it all."

"I know," I laughed. "I remember feeling like that, but I'm so used to it now. It's just become a part of who I am."

"Well, I don't think I will ever get used to it," he said, shaking his head.

I put my hand on his arm. "I'm so sorry you've gotten wrapped up in this, Zhao. I feel like you and your dad should have been given more of a chance to excuse yourself from it all."

"Are you kidding, Claire? This is unreal! This is some historical stuff! I wouldn't have missed being part of it for anything!"

I smiled at my good friend. "Well, I'm so glad I have you with me through all of this. I feel safer with you and your dad on board."

Twenty minutes later, Zhao and I entered the marbled foyer of the Officers Club. A beautiful fountain bubbled in the middle and Zhao paused with me, while I took a penny out of my clutch and made a wish.

From inside, piano music played, voices chattered, and glasses clinked. Zhao held out his arm and I slid my hand through. We both took a deep breath and walked through the double doors.

I'm pretty sure every officer and their wives, from every island in Hawaii had to be there. The ballroom was packed. Round, white clothed tables, with china plates and wine glasses outlined the large dance floor. Long buffet tables lined a row of glass French doors that led out into a beautiful lush garden, lit by dozens of tiki lights.

We followed the wall on the outside of the tables inconspicuously, not wanting to walk out in the middle of everyone who was on the dance floor talking, not dancing. Right in the middle of it all was Lt. General Gray. I did my best to avoid eye contact, get to a table in the corner, and hide as soon as I could. We had almost made it when Zhao lightly grabbed my arm.

"Claire, Lt. General is waving us over."

I looked into the swarm of faces and stopped when I saw his familiar face. He was waving at us and beside him a petite, brunette woman smiled just as big. I waved back, but he waved again motioning us over.

"Let's go," Zhao said, taking my hand and leading us through all the tables and people.

"Zhao! Haley!" Lt. General said when we at last

reached him. "I want you to meet my wife, Corrin."

I said hello and shook hands with his beautiful wife. Her smile was genuine and she seemed really excited to meet us. I wondered if Lt. General had told her anything about me.

"Hello Claire," she smiled sweetly. "Adam's told me so much about you."

"Hmmm, Adam," I thought to myself. *"Adam Gray."* It was always interesting to learn the first name of my fellow airmen, since we were on a last name basis all the time.

"It's so nice to meet you too. I love your dress," I smiled, admiring her beautiful yellow gown.

"Thank you! I hope you're liking Hawaii. We've been here five years and we just love it!"

Corrin and I spent the next half hour talking about Hawaii and my job in the Air Force. I couldn't be too sure, but from some of the things she said, I could tell she at least knew something. We were just finishing up our conversation about the best places to shop, when Captain Crew and another woman approached us.

"Hi Anna!" Corrin said, hugging the lady. "Anna Crew, I would like for you to meet Claire Haley."

"Hello Claire," Anna said, holding out her gloved hand for me to shake. "It's a pleasure meeting you," she smiled stiffly. "Grant has told me a lot about you."

"It's a pleasure to meet you," I said, keeping Captain Crew in my peripheral vision. He was talking to Lt. General and Zhao, but mainly just asking Zhao about his job in aeronautics and Houston.

"Girls! Girls!" Mrs. Crew's voice shreaked above the crowd. I followed her glare across the dance floor to two girls who were parading around several men, rubbing their arms and leaning in close to talk. I looked closer, and noticed Sgt. Mancuso talking to one of them, drink in hand, looking rather bored. I caught his eye and he smiled at me, rolling his eyes. I couldn't help but laugh at the karma being served up right in front of me. Sorry Mancuso, that's payback for all the hellish log hikes you've put me through.

"Kirsten! Kylie!" she yelled again, waving them over. This time one of the girls glanced our way, embarrassed and obviously not thrilled about her mom interrupting them. She rolled her eyes and grabbed her sister's arm, mumbling something. The other girl glanced at us, with a pouty look on her face. She turned to say something to the officer she was talking to, then followed her sister towards us.

I looked over at Corrin, who shook her head at me, obviously not thrilled to be seeing them. Kaena was right, I thought as I watched them march begrudgingly across the dance floor. What a hot mess.

"Girls, I want you to meet Claire," Anna smiled sweetly at them. "She is in your dad's company. Claire, these are our daughters Kirsten and Kylie, and of course girls, you know Mrs. Gray."

"Hello…" I began, stretching a hand out to shake their hands, but was quickly interrupted.

"Good evening Mrs. Gray," Kylie, the blonde, smiled

sweetly at her, completely ignoring me. "It's a pleasure to see you again."

"Kirsten," her mom nodded to the redhead, attempting to get her to say hello.

But Kirsten was having none of it.

"Oh come on, mom," she said, her words slurred and her eyes half closed. "You saw me over there." She pointed across the room, to the guys who seemed amused watching our conversation from afar. "You saw me talking to someone and you still interrupted. You know what you are?" she asked, raising her voice and swaying back and forth. "You're rude. Rude, rude mom!"

"Kirsten," Mrs. Crew said in a hushed voice. "Have you been drinking? This is so embarrassing for your father and I. Please stop."

Kirsten laughed loudly at her. "Oh, really? Really?" she almost yelled. "News flash mom! I didn't want to come to this boring ball anyway! All these old people everywhere."

"Kirsten Renee!" Captain Crew said, moving closer to us and grabbing her by the arm. "I swear young lady! I've had it with you."

Kirsten tried to wiggle her arm free from her dad's grasp. "Let go dad!!" she yelled.

Captain Crew grabbed her harder. "Kylie!" He looked around to find Kylie, who had made her way over to Zhao and was trying to strike up a conversation with him in the midst of all the chaos. "Kylie, take her home." He looked back over at Kirsten, "And that's where you better stay!"

"Grant, I'll take her," Mrs. Crew said, wrapping her arm around Kirsten's waist.

"No Anna," Captain Crew said. "You're not missing anything else, because of her bad choices."

"I'll be back," Anna said, looking over her shoulder, guiding Kirsten away.

We all watched in silence as the three of them left the ballroom.

"My apologies to you both," Captain Crew said looking at Zhao and me, his face flushed.

"It's no problem, Sir," Zhao said.

"It's fine, Sir," I echoed, surprised that he apologized.

The group of people that had been around us and witnessed the scene unfold, went back to talking as did Zhao, Lt. General, Captain Crew, and Sgt. Mancuso, who joined them after the girls left.

"Crew, I told you what I'd do if that was my daughter," Mancuso said, and then acted as if he were kicking a football.

Lt. General laughed, "Sure, Mancuso. I'm sure Grant wants to take advice from some thirty something, who's never parented anyone in his life."

"I feel so sorry for Anna," Corrin said to me quietly. "Kirsten has some serious issues."

"Yeah, it looks like she had a little too much to drink," I said.

"Oh, she wasn't drunk Claire. It's a little more severe than that." She lowered her voice even more. "She has a drug issue. Her parents have tried many times to get her help to no avail. She thinks she's indestructible."

"People with drug issues usually do," I said looking over at Captain Crew. My heart was so sad for him. No wonder why he walked around with a chip on his shoulder all the time. My mom was right. You should always show kindness, especially since you never know what someone is going through.

Zhao and I spent the rest of the night meeting a ton of officers and then eating as much food as we could hold. I ate two plates and I'm pretty sure Zhao had at least five. I stopped counting after the fifth one, because I think I gained five extra pounds just watching him.

Later that night, I walked out onto my balcony. I was a little bummed I didn't get to go to my island tonight, but the ball wasn't so bad. I looked up at the bright starry sky, filled with puffs of white cotton ball clouds, illuminated by the moon. I wanted so badly to fly up and over the clouds and watch them float underneath me, but I was so tired. This whole week I had spent flying at the airfield and it took a lot of energy out of me.

My phone rang inside my apartment. I was thrilled to see Alicia's name pop up.

"Mony?!"

"Claire!" she yelled excitedly into the phone. "Finally! Where have you been? I've been trying to call you and snap you for two days!"

"Are you sure?" I asked, checking my phone. "I don't see your number on my missed calls list and as far as snap goes, that's hit or miss."

"Of course, I'm sure! What has you so busy that you can't call me? You're too good for me now, Miss Airman Supergirl?" she laughed.

"Of course not," I giggled. "I miss you like crazy, Mony. How is the wedding planning going?"

Alicia sighed into the phone. "Honestly Claire, I haven't been doing too much. I've been so busy with school, I haven't had the time. Plus, I don't know...it's just not the same without you and now that Shawn left, all I want to do is lay in bed all day."

"Oh Mony, I know it's hard, but you have to get busy. June will be here before you know it and busyness is the perfect remedy for depression."

"I know, but I have zero motivation. I miss Shawn so much. I worry about him constantly."

"When did he leave?"

"Ten days ago."

"I'm so sorry," I said, my heart aching also, at the thought of Johnny. "I miss Johnny so much too, but at least they're together and not alone."

"True," she agreed. "Have you heard from Johnny?"

"I finally got a text from him this week. He said he's had no service, so get ready for that."

"This is miserable, Claire. Do you know not a day has gone by that I haven't talked to Shawn since we met?"

"Trust me, I know," I said sympathetically.

"I wish you were here. You're the only one I can talk to who knows exactly what I'm going through, plus you have such great ideas. I would love to have your input on my wedding planning."

My mind raced quickly trying to find some way to cheer her up. "You know what, Mony? I can still help with planning the wedding. We can just do it over facetime. I know it's not the same, but at least it's something."

Alicia was quiet for a moment. "I didn't think about that."

"Sure!" I said, "And we can get Kass and Lexi in on it. That way we can all talk more!"

So, Alicia and I decided that every Thursday night at 9 pm their time, we would spend 30 minutes on wedding planning, bouncing ideas off each other. That seemed to cheer her up alot and I was already looking forward to next Thursday.

THIRTY

MONDAY NIGHT, DR. Zhao joined us at the airfield once again, having just flown back to the island from the mainland.

"So how was the ball?" he asked as they suited me up.

(Now, they had me wearing this weird suit with all these wires on it. Have you ever seen someone get filmed for a video game and they have to wear those suits that record their every move? That's what I had on. A motion button at every curve on my body.)

"It was actually pretty ok," Zhao said snapping another monitor on the ankle of my suit. "The food was amazing."

"Did you get pictures?"

"A few," I replied to Dr. Zhao, pulling out my phone and showing him.

Dr. Zhao laughed at our stupid pics. "It definitely looks like you had a great time."

Lt. General Gray joined us and we jumped in a van to head out to the furthest landing strip, closest to the ocean. The dark sky above was almost completely covered by low clouds rolling in from the west.

"Well, no one will be able to see you tonight for sure," Zhao said looking up at the sky.

"We only have about an hour out here tonight. There's a pretty bad storm a couple of hours out and I want you guys back on base before it gets here," Lt. General Gray warned us. He then got on his radio and ordered the lights shut off on our runway.

Dr. Zhao was busy clicking away on his laptop set up at his makeshift desk in the van. "Ok! We're a go!" he said looking up from his keyboard.

I walked out onto the airstrip, turned and gave Zhao a wink, then shot into the sky. I looked down and watched them disappear as the low clouds quickly enveloped me.

"Sparrow, do you copy?" Lt. General asked into my headphones. (Sparrow was the code name they had given me for the radio, while they answered to GC, short for Ground Command.)

"Go ahead GC," I replied. My goodness, he was already checking in and I just left.

"Go up to 250 and stop so we can get some readings on you."

"Roger that," I replied.

I looked down at the height gauge strapped on my

wrist. 150 ft. Only 100 feet more to go. The wind whipped around, pushing me a little off my flight path. This was nothing new. I had found myself in plenty of wind patterns that would get me off course. I focused on my vertical compass and tried my best to stay in the flight path that stretched directly above the airfield. The trip up took a little longer than usual, as I fought against the wind.

"GC, I have reached altitude level and holding."

"Copy that Sparrow," Zhao's voice echoed into my head phones.

Now to just wait while they monitor whatever it was they were monitoring. The early September wind cut through my flight suit and I sat with my legs crossed Indian style, wishing I had thrown on a sweatshirt. I looked at my watch. It was well past 11 pm.

I yawned into my mic and watched the clouds roll beneath. The wind steadily became harsher as it blew in a straight line path. I turned and faced the east, hoping to catch a glimpse of the moon that would peak through the sky momentarily.

"Sparrow, can you give me a reading on your tat," Zhao asked.

"Copy," I replied, looking down at my Saturn tat. "It's holding steady at 7."

"Clear."

For some reason they were keeping a scale of my tat readings. The brighter pink my tat was, the stronger my energy level and heart rate.

I sat calmly in the air as the wind speed picked up again. Lt. General said the storm wouldn't be here for another couple of hours, so I didn't worry about that. I thought about my conversation last night with Alicia and how bad I felt for her. I knew how she was feeling, because I missed Johnny so much. I hate to admit it, but I was struggling with bitterness toward him. Something inside was telling me he was making no effort to contact me. I know that's not fair with no proof, but I think that's a typical girl thought. We tend to think the worst, but at the end of the day I kept telling myself he was in a deadzone and it was as simple as that.

A few drops of rain hit my cheek sideways, erasing Johnny's face from my eyes as I focused on the clouds. They had grown even more dense and I could barely see around me.

"Claire! Claire!" Zhao yelled into my headphones.

Why was he using my name? We had been specifically ordered to use our code names.

"Go ahead, *GC*," I said emphasizing the GC to remind him to call me Sparrow.

"Abort! Abort immediately!"

I froze for a moment, not sure of what I had just heard.

"Did you copy? Abort immediately!! WATERSPOUT! WATERSPOUT AT 7 O CLOCK!"

I turned to my left, facing where the wind was coming from. About 60 feet away, a giant waterspout was making its way quickly toward me. I looked up at this incredible sight, made visible only by the moon's reflection bouncing off it.

The tunnel stretched high into the clouds, funneling out at the top. Though terrifying, it was one of the most majestic things I had ever seen. My eyes froze on it, almost in a trance.

"Sparrow!" I heard Lt. General's voice boom through my headphones again. "Abort! Return immediately!"

I mentally told my body to drop to earth and felt gravity begin to pull me down, but it was too late. The outside winds circled viciously around as the spout grabbed my 115 pound frame and pulled me into the violent rotation. I tried to kick and push my way out to no avail. Water being pulled up from the ocean stung my face, as my headphones were ripped away and flung into the dark night. The wind whipped my body around, as I was tossed upside down and sideways. Breathing was almost impossible with the rate of speed I was going, and a sharp pain ripped through my side as my body flipped one way and then the total opposite in an instant. I screamed out in pain and curled myself into a ball, covering my head with my hands, hoping to shield myself from the violent winds.

"Oh God, please help me," I whispered, as I tumbled in the vortex. My fingers found the ring Johnny had given to me and I held onto it for dear life.

After what seemed like forever, a miracle happened. The winds slowed down and I pushed against the vortex with all my might, trying to fly out. At last I broke free and it spat me out into the open sky, as I cartwheeled through the air and finally came to a stop. I watched in wonder, as it slowly moved away and finally dissipated into the air. The wind cut through me and I caught my breath in shock, thanking God I was alive. There is no way I should have survived that. I was drenched, missing a shoe and my headset, with my long wet curls matted around my face.

Now to find my way back to the air base. I rubbed my blurry eyes that were overly sensitive after the salt water bullets had pounded them and looked for any sign of light. In the distance, the lights of the air traffic control tower and runways blinked in unison. I couldn't believe how far I had been pulled away from it, at least three miles out.

I leaned into flying mode and felt a stabbing pain in my ribs again. It was so sharp, I had to breathe shallow. I tucked my arm against my side and began flying to our dark runway. As I approached, someone frantically yelled into the night.

"Claire! Claaairree!!!" Zhao yelled above the crashing waves.

A little further down, Lt. General was scanning the water with a bright flashlight.

I landed out of sight and down the beach in the darkness, just in case someone was there I didn't know about. I walked towards the guys, the pain in my side keeping me from yelling to them.

"Let's call in the Coast Guard!" Lt. General Gray frantically commanded.

I picked up my pace to get closer. There was no way I wanted the Coast Guard in on this one, afterall, how do you explain getting sucked into a waterspout? Lt. General walked toward the van, while Zhao continued to pace back and forth on the beach yelling my name.

"Zhao!" I yelled out, but he didn't hear me.

"Claire!" he yelled again.

"Zhao, calm down!" Lt. General yelled over his shoulder.

"Zhao! Right here!" I tried again.

Zhao turned in my direction. I waved one arm as high as I could and he finally spotted me.

"Oh my god, Claire! Lt. General! She's here!"

Lt. General and Dr. Zhao jumped from the van and ran over to me.

I limped towards them in the thick sand, trying to find my balance with a shoe missing, a possible cracked rib, and sheer exhaustion.

Zhao and Lt. General came on either side of me, each one grabbing an arm to stabilize me.

"Not there, please!" I shrieked as Zhao pulled my arm up. I pulled it down again close to my side. "I think it's broken."

"Omg, Claire!" Zhao yelled into my ear. "What happened to you? We thought you got sucked into the waterspout!"

"I did," I said calmly, as all three of them stopped and looked at me.

Lt. General scooped me up in his arms, careful not

to hurt my ribs. "Zhao, grab all the equipment. We're going to the hospital."

THIRTY-ONE

RAIN WAS PELTING against my slider door, when I finally made it home at 2 a.m.

"You gonna be ok?" Zhao asked, as I slowly sat on the couch.

"Yeah Zhao, thank you. It's just a bruised rib, so it should heal up pretty fast."

"What did Major Wang say about recovery time?" he asked sitting beside me.

"He said a week of bed rest and we'll go from there."

"That sounds terrible," he laughed. "You're almost impossible to keep still."

"For real," I smiled at him. "This is going to be miserable."

"Well, what matters most is you getting better. Do you need anything? I can go to the store tomorrow."

"No thanks, Zhao. Luckily, I went yesterday."

He said good night, reminding me again to call him if I needed anything. As soon as he left, I got in the shower, then fell into a restless night's sleep. Not only was my side hurting with every turn, I couldn't escape the howling noise of the vortex in my mind.

The next few days, I slept almost constantly, between the many phone calls I received from my mom and Kass. I was even surprised to get a call from Major Silva. That was a little weird. I felt like he was checking in on me, not in an authoritative kind of way, but more of a fatherly one. Kass was right. Something was definitely going on with all that, but I was perfectly ok with it. Major Silva was so kind to me.

By Thursday evening, I was delirious with some major cabin fever. I sat in my chair just inside my apartment, watching the sunset with the slider open. Out on the back lawn, the guys had started a game of volleyball and I watched as the ball popped into view from my perch. They were yelling and talking smack to each other, overly celebrating a spike or point win. I didn't mind though. I loved hearing them. They were so funny.

After a while the sun was gone and the dark, quietness of the night slowly crept in around me. I put the book I was reading down and headed into the kitchen to get something to eat. I made a sub sandwich, then out of habit grabbed a baggie to pack it in, my ritual when spending the day at my island.

I stared down at the sub and baggie. A salty, warm breeze blew into my room and I walked out onto my patio, looking out into the dark night. I felt an incredible urge to go to the island. I hadn't been in two weeks and it was driving me crazy. Tomorrow would be Friday and everyone would be working. Since I didn't have to go back to the doctor until Monday, I knew the chances of anyone checking on me were slim and I could get away with it.

"You could totally get away with it, Claire," I told myself as I went back into the kitchen to make a second sub to take, just in case I went. "I mean, it's not like they told you that you couldn't fly..." I stopped, realizing I was talking to myself. The cabin fever was beginning to get to me. I had to get out.

I packed my bag in anticipation of the next morning, again, just in case. I could always change my mind last minute, right?

By 9 a.m. the next morning, I was stretched out on my comforter, on the slab of rock, soaking up the warm sunshine and listening to my Michael Buble playlist, as always. The waves flowed gently up the beach, their beautiful song lulling me into a peaceful nap.

At ten my alarm woke me, and I popped into the air

over the island, just to make sure the drug pirates had not returned. When the coast was all clear, I would float back down and nap again or read, checking every hour as a precaution.

My day was once again so perfect. I got through my book by early afternoon and sat back to watch a school of dolphins bouncing in and out of the waves, as Peter Cetera's "Glory of Love" filled the air around me. Oh, how I wish I could be out there with them. I walked the beach, adding some beautiful sand dollars and shark teeth to my already impressive collection.

I had also been pretty lucky at finding pearls. Maybe I could get enough to make mom a real pearl necklace, instead of the imitation one Kass and I had given her on her birthday.

The sun was slowly going down, when I decided to do my area check one last time. I threw my binoculars around my neck, popped casually into the air, and was just getting over the highest point of the island when I heard music. I dropped down in the middle of the brush and headed for my tall, hidden palm tree, on the peak of the hill above the cave. The small boat wasn't on the beach, but just beyond the reef, the Sydney Jo bobbled on the waves, its deck full of people in swimsuits, dancing and talking loudly.

My eyes peered through my binoculars for signs of anyone coming to the island, but the little dingy boat they had used the last time was secured firmly to the side of the boat. The yacht was so close, I could see the faces of the people, but no sign of Phantom and the crew he had accompanied to the beach the last time. Then something caught my attention. Poking out from a sea of brunettes, a sharp red haired woman appeared from below deck. I looked at her curiously, as she stuck out like a sore thumb with her pale skin in the mix of all the dark haired, tan bodies. She laughed louder than everyone else and at some point sounded like she was yelling at someone. She appeared to be drunk as she stumbled around the deck, at last finding a seat, her face in the dead center of my binoculars.

I gasped. "Kirsten. Kirsten Crew," I whispered.

THIRTY-TWO

INSTEAD OF WATCHING the sunset, I kept my eyes on the yacht, following Kirsten's every move. She bent over a table with her male companion, snorting up some kind of drug, then stumbled around the deck, sometimes dancing and at one point almost falling overboard.

I waited until the sun set completely, then flew out of the palm tree to my rock to gather my things. The moonlight sparkled on the waves, as I slid on my chucks and slowly pulled my sweatshirt over my head, tucking an elbow in one sleeve to use as a makeshift sling. This would secure it during flight to keep too much movement from around my ribs. I grabbed my backpack and slowly took off into the sky, getting safely out of sight of the Sydney Jo, still anchored in the same spot. I flew high above and hovered over the boat that was now a tiny light against the dark ocean's surface.

I thought about Captain Crew and his wife. They were probably at home worried about Kirsten at this very moment. I felt bad about leaving her there, but she didn't seem to be in any danger with them. Actually, they all seemed like friends.

I turned and headed for base. On the trip home I thought about my mom and how devastated she would be if this was me or any of my sisters. We were far from perfect, but at least she never had to deal with us getting involved in any of that garbage. I could never do that to her. She has been through enough already.

I landed down the beach where I knew no one would be and peeked through the tree line that divided my barracks from the sand. When the coast was clear, I scurried up the bank and through the PT yard. I was just getting ready to fly up to my balcony when a familiar voice stopped me.

"What are you doing, Haley?"

I jumped in surprise, as my eyes adjusted to the darkness, and a figure emerged from the shadow of the building.

"Sgt. Mancuso," I said, my voice shaking. One second later and he would have witnessed me fly to the balcony. How could I have been so careless?

"What are you doing?" he asked again.

I let out a big sigh trying to think of something.

"I...I dropped something from my...my ummm…" I pointed upward trying to remember the word.

"Balcony?" he asked curiously.

"Yeah," I blushed. "Balcony."

"What did you drop?"

"Ummm...a ring," I lied.

"A ring?" he laughed. "Do you think you'll be able to find a ring out here tonight, carrying around a big backpack?"

I looked at my backpack, then at the ground. "Probably not, Sir."

He smiled at me, shaking his head. "Well, you're supposed to be nursing that shoulder. I'm not going to ask you where you've been, but let's just make sure this doesn't happen again, ok?"

I smiled back at him, relieved to be off the hook. "Thank you, Sgt. Mancuso."

"You're welcome, Haley. Good night."

"Good night," I replied, turning quickly and heading inside. I breathed a sigh of relief. Could you imagine what would have happened if he had seen me?

My hands shook nervously at the thought of that, while I tried to get my key in the door.Once inside my apartment, I set everything on the bed and caught my breath, as a bit of depression crept in around me. I was not happy to be back in my room. The thought of spending another whole week here alone, made my heart sink and as far as sneaking out again, well that was not going to happen. I had a feeling Mancuso would be watching now.

My phone rang a familiar sound. I knew it was my

mom before I even picked it up.

"Mom!" I almost yelled in my excitement. "Hey! How are you?"

"Hi, sweet darling," she said, her usual greeting to me. My heart melted when I heard her voice. I missed her so much. "How are you doing? Momma thought I would call because I was just thinking about you."

"I'm okay," I told her, even though I didn't feel ok. It's so crazy how she knows to call at just the right time. "Everything's good here."

"How are your ribs? Are they still very sore?" she asked, concerned.

"Oh, they're fine, mom," I said, laying gently on the bed to avoid them hurting more. "They are healing up real fast." That wasn't quite the truth. They were healing better before I flew today. I didn't think flying would bother me much, but I should have known better. On take off my body feels like it's being shot out of a cannon, the momentum of gravity leaving, squeezing around me. I felt it even more so today on take off.

"You're not out flying are you?" she pressed further.

I was quiet for a moment. I didn't want to lie, but I didn't want to worry her either. Too late.

"Claire," she sighed. "I thought they made it clear, you are not to fly unless under their direction."

"I know mom, but I'm so bored...plus you know how much I love it."

"Claire, the sooner you heal up and follow their orders, the sooner you can get home." I was quiet, because I knew she was right. "You don't want to run the risk of getting hurt worse or...or someone discovering your secret. Don't you agree?"

"Yes, Ma'am. You're right." I sighed.

"Good," she said. "Stay out of the sky, Wonder Woman."

"Wonder Woman is lame, Mom," I laughed. "She doesn't fly. Try Supergirl."

"Excuse me, Supergirl," she giggled.

"How's everything back home?" I asked.

"Well, speaking of Supergirl, your popularity has reached a fever pitch around here lately."

"What are you talking about?" I asked, sitting up in bed. "My popularity?"

"Yes!" Mom exclaimed. "It's crazy around here, Claire. People have come from all over just to try and catch a sighting of you. They've been camping out at the bridge and hanging out at the various locations you've been spotted."

My eyes grew wide and I gasped. This was insane. "Are you serious, mom?"

"Oh yes!" she exclaimed. "You should see all the Supergirl collectibles they have. You're all over the mall and in stores everywhere. They even made the Supergirl look like you, long brown curly hair and all."

This was so crazy and mom actually sounded excited about it.

"That's insane mom!" I said, a little nervous, but more thrilled. "I can't even believe that."

"It's true," she said. "But you know Claire, all this happening here, makes me feel even better that you're there, at least until it all can simmer down. Any girl with long curly brown hair is being looked at and questioned by the authorities. Some of them are followed by people thinking they are you.I feel safer knowing you're well protected. Sebastian tells me you are with one of the toughest units in the whole Air Force."

"I am mom," I reassured her. "So don't worry about anything. He's right. I'm well protected."

I heard mom breathe a sigh of relief and that made me so happy.

"That's a big worry off my shoulders baby...and I know you'll make good decisions. You always have."

"Thanks, mom. I love you," I smiled.

"I love you, too. Is there anything I can do or get for you? I'm getting a package ready to send you."

"Ummm," I thought for a moment. "How about one of those Supergirl tee shirts?"

"Done," she laughed.

THIRTY-THREE

SATURDAY NIGHT, ZHAO came over with a big cheese pizza and a bag full of junk food. We sat on my couch with the pizza between us, to binge watch the *Karate Kid* movies. I couldn't believe Zhao had never seen them before.

"So guess who I saw yesterday," Zhao said later as we started the *Karate Kid 2* and he threw the empty pizza box in the garbage.

"Who?"

"Kylie Crew," he said rolling his eyes.

"How did that happen?" I laughed.

Zhao sat back down on the couch. "Captain Crew brought her to the admin building this week when I was there with my dad."

"Oh no," I giggled. "How did that go?"

"Claire, she's so wild. She was flirting with me and asking all kinds of questions about my job. It was so uncomfortable." He shook his head. "Those girls. The Crews have their hands full."

"Yes, they do," I agreed.

We started the movie and I could see Zhao was really enjoying it. I toyed with the idea of telling him that I had seen Kirsten, but if I did that, I would have to tell him about my island. A part of me thought it would be good for someone to know, just in case something happened and I was trapped there. The other part of me feared someone else finding out and that I would lose the freedom I had to go whenever I wanted. I kept arguing with myself through the whole movie on whether or not to tell him. In the movie, Daniel was just getting ready to break the ice in the bar scene, when I finally decided.

I grabbed the remote and paused the movie, just as Daniel dramatically raised his hand to karate chop the ice.

Zhao looked at me wide-eyed. "What are you doing Claire?" he asked emphatically, with a mouth full of popcorn. "He's going to break the ice!"

"I know, but I have to tell you something," I said seriously.

"Oh no," Zhao laughed. "The last time you had to tell me something serious, I found out you can fly. What is it now? You have X-ray vision?"

"Nooo," I smiled. "I have to tell you something about Kirsten."

"Ok." I had his attention now.

"I saw her yesterday."

"She came here?" he asked.

"No. I saw her…" I took a deep breath. "I saw her out on the ocean."

Zhao sat in silence for a moment. "Well, explain please," he said at last.

I told Zhao everything. I started at the beginning with me finding the island and how I had been there every weekend. I told him about the drug pirates and at last about Kirsten. I even showed him a video of my island and the footage I had taken of the drugs, the Sydney Jo, and Kirsten.

Zhao sat up and leaned forward, resting his chin in his hands in deep thought.

"Wow, Claire. This is a hard one. I mean, you can't really tell anyone without them asking how you got out there, but at the same time I fear for Kirsten's safety. She's only 17, you know."

"She is? I thought she was at least 20."

"Oh no. She's still in high school."

I thought about Kass and how she was only 18. I couldn't imagine her being in that position, out on a boat in the middle of nowhere with a bunch of drug smugglers.

"Zhao, I have to do something before something bad happens to her."

"I know," he agreed. "We'll figure it out."

I spent the rest of the weekend and into the next week healing up. On Friday, Lt. General Gray finally gave me the ok to go out, first to a meeting at his office and then The Shack, but only if I watched. No participation. I didn't care though. I was just excited to get out of my room.

"So, you haven't been flying this week, have you?" Zhao asked as we rode together on the shuttle to the admin building.

I shot him a warning look. He was talking a little too loud for the driver to hear.

"Oh sorry," he whispered covering his mouth. "I forget sometimes."

"It's ok," I whispered back. "I do it too and no, I promise I haven't. I want to get better."

"How does flying affect your ribs?" he asked. "I mean, does it make you breathe heavy or something?"

"No," I laughed, being as quiet as I could. "I don't know. It's hard to explain, but on take off it's like...it's like you're being shot out of a cannon and the pressure you feel against your body as the gravity leaves, well you feel every ounce of it. The return is a little different. That's like you're falling, and then all of a sudden the air around you just closes in and you feel it tighten against your body as the gravity returns. I don't know, you just feel pressure everywhere... apparently a lot on the ribs too."

Zhao stared at me wide-eyed.

"What?" I laughed.

"You're just amazing. I still can't believe it."

I smiled at him and squeezed his arm. "Thank you, but I'm sorry you're caught up in my crazy world, Zhao."

"I'm not sorry," he said smiling back.

Forty five minutes later, Zhao and I sat outside Lt. General's office with Major Wang waiting for our meeting that should have started 30 minutes ago. Lt. General's office door was closed and inside we could hear heavy talking and a female voice sobbing. Zhao and I looked anxiously at each other.

Moments later Lt. General, Captain Crew and Anna Crew, along with three Security Force Officers emerged from the office. Anna held a tissue up by her eyes in a failed attempt to cover her tears, but nothing could hide her swollen, red face.

"We'll get on this immediately," one of the SF Officers promised them. Captain Crew and Anna followed the officers out, while Lt. General motioned us into his office. We found our seats across from his desk.

"Captain Crew won't be joining us today," he said as he shut the door. He paused for a moment as though he was thinking about what he wanted to tell us. "Umm, one of his daughters is missing. He's on his way to file a missing person's report."

"Which one?" I blurted out without thinking.

"Kirsten."

Zhao looked over at me, then quickly back at Lt.

General. "For how long?" he asked.

"Well, today is Friday...since Tuesday. So this is the third day."

I felt my heart sink and a chill run through my body that made me shiver.

"She's done this before, hasn't she? Ran away?" Major Wang asked. He was good friends with Captain Crew, so I was sure he had heard all kinds of stories.

Lt. General sat on the edge of his desk. "Well yeah, but this time is different. This time they got a ransom note."

The three of us audibly gasped at the same time. A ransom note to me, meant she was more than likely with the drug smugglers.

Lt. General continued, "Yeah, so we're contacting the FBI now, because a missing person case we can handle, but a ransom is something we need to pass on to them."

We sat in silence for a moment. Lt. General and Major Wang stared at the floor, while Zhao looked at me and then nodded at Lt. General as if he wanted me to tell him what I knew. I quickly gave him the universal sign for "no way" with my eyes and looked away quickly.

Zhao cleared his throat and my heart dropped. I just knew he was going to tell on me. "So...what did the ransom note say?" he asked, to my relief.

"Well...you can't share this with anyone, but they have until sundown Sunday night to get the money where it's supposed to go, but that's all the details I can share."

I shook my head, dumbfounded. "This is so stupid. Who does ransoms anymore?"

"Someone pretty desperate," Major Wang replied, "and that's what's so scary about it."

THIRTY-FOUR

THE REST OF the work day we spent at the shack. I tried to focus on watching Professor Corral and Zhao, but all I could think about was Kirsten. I knew she had to be on the Sidney Jo. Where else would they take her?

Later that evening, after we had finished with Professor Corral, Zhao walked me up to my room.

"Zhao, I can't stop thinking about Kirsten," I confessed. "I just know they have her on the Sidney Jo."

"Ok Claire, but what if she is? There's nothing you can do, other than tell Lt. General."

I nodded my head in agreement with him, as I fiddled with the key in my door. "I just feel sorry for the Crews. I think about Kass and how I would move heaven and earth to go rescue her."

Zhao folded his arms and looked at me skeptically.

"What are you saying, Claire?"

"I wanna go get her, Zhao. I know she must be terrified."

I opened the door and Zhao gently grabbed my arm, pulling me inside and shutting it behind us. "Are you crazy? No Claire! The FBI has this, now let them handle it."

"In forty eight hours?" I exclaimed, tossing my keys on the counter. "You think they're going to find her in that vast ocean in forty eight hours?"

"No, but they do have a better chance if you tell Lt. General what you know. At least they'll know where to start."

I bit the side of my lip in frustration. "Zhao, you know as well as I do, he'll put me on lock down in this room if he finds out I've been flying. Then I won't be able to help at all."

Zhao slid his glasses up his nose, the way he always did when he was frustrated. "I can't let you, Claire. It's just too dangerous."

I placed my hands on his shoulders and looked into his eyes. "Zhao, I'm just going to find the yacht and see if she's on it. That's it. I...I won't engage with them. Come on, please? Please? We've gotta do something."

I thought I had him, but then he answered with a curt, "Not at the risk of you getting hurt. I'm not doing it."

I sat down on the couch, fuming. I appreciated Zhao's concern for me, but I wish I had never told him about my island adventures. Zhao was my best buddy here, but there was no way I was going to let him stop me.

"Zhao, it's like this. I'm going and you can either help me, or just back off and let me do it all myself."

Zhao almost laughed and sat down beside me. "Well, I'll just go tell Lt. General what you're doing and see how quickly he stops you."

"Fine," I said snidely. "You go right ahead. I'll be out of here before you can even get to his office."

Zhao stared at me, knowing I was right and there was nothing he could say to stop me. "Claire, please don't."

I gave him my defiant "*I'm not giving up*" stare.

"Whatever Claire," he said, suddenly jumping up off the couch. "Go ahead and get yourself in trouble with the higher ups or even worse...killed. I don't want anything to do with this!"

He grabbed his stuff and marched to the door, slamming it dramatically behind him. I stared at the closed door for a moment, then sat back on the couch to think about what I was doing. Was he right? Should I be risking my life for someone who could care less about mine or her own for that matter? But then... then I remembered who I was. I was an airman in the United States Air Force. This was my life. I was trained to fight and if necessary, give my life for my country and sometimes that included people who could care less.

A soft knock at the door interrupted my thoughts. I opened it to find a bashful faced Zhao standing there.

"Fine," he sighed. "At least if I help, I'll know where you are and what you're doing and I won't worry myself to death."

"Thanks Zhao," I said, jumping into his arms.

"Yeah, yeah," he replied, playfully rolling his eyes and shutting the door behind him. "Alright, what do you have in mind?"

"Well… I was thinking. After sundown tonight, I'm going to fly out to the island and look for the Sydney Jo. I just want to see if she's on there. From what I remember, there are windows everywhere, so I can just look inside for her without being seen."

"And what if the Sydney Jo's not at the island? You promise you'll come right back?"

"Well, if it's not there, I should probably just stay all day and wait until tomorrow night. You know, just in case it comes during the day tomorrow."

"Claire, that's too long for you to be gone," he argued.

"Zhao, you're forgetting I do this all the time. I always leave and stay the day."

He sighed loudly and buried his head in his hands in frustration. "You said you have no service out there? How am I supposed to stay in touch with you?"

"I have that figured out. We'll just have to use our radios."

"Our radios? Claire, are you crazy? Then anyone can pick us up out there."

"We'll only use them in an emergency, otherwise, I'll try my best to reach you by phone. You have your radio, right?"

"Yes," Zhao said annoyed, then turned to me, grabbing

my hands. "Look Claire, if we're going to do this, I want to plan it out right. You going tonight is too soon."

I made us something to eat, then Zhao and I sat at my kitchenette table planning the next two days out. We decided that I would leave early in the morning, so I wouldn't have to spend two nights there. I didn't mind staying two nights, but I felt like I had to give Zhao some sort of compromise to make him feel like he had a little bit of control.

"The less time you have to be out there alone, the better," he said.

I suppose he was right to some extent. The battery on my phone and on the radio would only last for so long. I was to keep my phone on and only use the radio when I spotted the Sydney Jo and to check in occasionally. We even made up new radio names, so as not to draw suspicion from Lt. General. I was "Flygirl" and he was "Kyoto" after his home city in Japan. We found a channel that was never used and decided to stick with that. Zhao was going to hunker down for the weekend in his room gaming, as he waited to hear from me.

I packed a duffle bag instead of my regular backpack, because I had so much more to carry. I had to pack the radio, plus any extra food and supplies I would need in case I got stuck.

"Remember, check in with me during our scheduled times so I know you're ok," Zhao said, standing at the door of my apartment. It was well past midnight and we were exhausted.

"I promise I will," I yawned. He wrapped his arms around me and kissed the top of my head.

"I swear, if anything happens to you, I'll never forgive myself and neither will anyone else for that matter."

"I promise I'll be fine," I reassured him.

In the dark early hours the next morning, I launched off the roof of my barracks, my duffle bag strapped behind me and headed for my island. The late September air was extra thick above the ocean, so by the time I arrived I was drenched. I flew over the north side of the island where the Sydney Jo was last anchored, but there was no sign of the yacht anywhere.

I landed softly on my rock, the silence around me deafening, except the steady lapping of the waves rolling on the beach. I grabbed my big soft towel and dried my face, thankful I had put my hair in a bun. Peeling off my wet clothes was a challenge, as I tried my best not to strain my ribs that were already a little sore from the flight with the duffle. The ocean breeze collided with my wet skin sending a chill over my body. I dried off quickly and wrapped the towel around me, then shuffled through the duffle for my sweats and a warm sweatshirt and put them on as quickly as possible.

The next few hours I layed on my blanket, falling asleep for a while at one point. Every thirty minutes I would set my alarm and pop into the air, looking for any signs of the yacht, but to my disappointment, the ocean's flat surface spread out empty before me.

At noon I pulled out my radio and turned it on. I clicked it three times and paused, then clicked it three times more, my code for checking in with Zhao. To my delight, the radio clicked three times back. These little babies had some serious range.

After some radio static, I heard Zhao's voice. "Flygirl from Kyoto, I will be attempting to contact you via TX (phone)."

I was so excited to hear his voice. "Clear Kyoto."

I stared down at my phone anxiously awaiting Zhao's call, but after five minutes had passed and I hadn't heard from him, I knew it wasn't going to work.

"Well, you knew that was a long shot, Claire," I said to myself.

The radio, after some static, came back to life again. *"Flygirl from Kyoto."*

"Go ahead, Kyoto."

"Tx is out of range. What's your status?"

"I'm 10-4."

"Any signs of the target?" he pressed further.

"That's a negative," I responded, trying to be as vague as I possibly could. I felt pretty confident that this channel was a ghost channel, but you could never be too sure.

"Clear. I'll contact you again at 1500."

"Clear."

I laid back to watch the large white clouds blow over. It was noon, but I wasn't feeling hungry yet. I couldn't stop thinking about Kirsten. What a brat, but still she was their daughter and a sister and I couldn't imagine what the Crews were thinking or doing right now.

The one thing I didn't know, nor could I have ever guessed, was that Zhao wasn't the only one listening to our radio transactions. Our "ghost" station was in fact an extra emergency frequency for the United States Coast Guard, and of course of all days they would have to tune in to it, it would be today.

THIRTY-FIVE

TODAY WAS ELLA Pearson's eighth birthday. More than anything, she loved fishing. So it was on this same Saturday that I had set out to find Kirsten, that Ella's father had rented a small charter boat to spend the day fishing off the southern coast of Oahu. Mid-morning the boat began to take on water and they were forced to abandon ship in a small inflatable raft. Ella's father was able to make one last SOS transmission before the boat was a total loss. The Coast Guard picked up the SOS, but by the time they reached Ella and her dad's last known location, their raft was gone, having been drug further out into the ocean by a strong southerly current.

At 11:30, the coast guard switched momentarily to our channel and within 30 minutes had located the raft. All personnel participating in the search were ordered back to the regular channel when Ella and her dad were secure, however one boat crew had forgotten to switch back over. That's where Zhao and I come into this little story. At noon, our transmission went over their radio, and out of curiosity, they left one radio on our channel for the rest of their shift. Zhao and I had missed all of their radio traffic in an attempt to conserve my batteries, something we should have thought about. How could we have been so stupid?

At two, I flew up again, binoculars in hand to scope out the ocean. Everything was clear, except to the southwest where a large shipping vessel was steadily going by. I relaxed knowing it was far enough away to not see me and had no plans of stopping at this little island.

I floated back down and turned on my radio, then did our three click code, smiling when Zhao clicked back.

"Flygirl from Kyoto."

"Go ahead, Kyoto."

"Any sign of the vessel?"

"That's a negative."

"Clear, if you get a visual, please contact me before you attempt a rescue."

"10-4. I'll contact you again at 1600."

The rest of the day went off without a hitch. I continued to update Zhao every two hours like I promised I would. I was disappointed when the sun went down and I hadn't seen any sign of the Sydney Jo. I ate dinner and then settled into my sleeping bag on the rock to watch the stars move across the sky. By midnight, my eyes were heavy and I drifted into a peaceful sleep.

At 3 a.m. I woke with a start. In the distance a ship's fog horn cut through the dark night, the wind whistled through the palm trees, and the waves on the shore grew larger with every strong breeze. I threw on my sweatshirt and popped into the air really quick, expecting to see nothing but blackness and even leaving the binoculars down on the rock. To my surprise lights glistened on the water on the north side. I rubbed my eyes, to make sure I was seeing what I thought was there.

The Sydney Jo bobbled peacefully on the water, almost like a mirage, but I knew this was the real deal.

I glided back down to my rock to catch my breath. This was it. Showtime. I grabbed the radio and turned it on, then clicked quickly, eagerly awaiting Zhao's reply.

"Come on Zhao," I whispered to myself.

At last he clicked back.

"*Kyoto from Flygirl*," I said, trying not to sound overly anxious.

"*Go ahead Flygirl.*"

"*Kyoto, be advised the vessel is in sight.*"

Zhao was quiet for a moment. "*Clear flygirl. Umm… will you be making contact with them?*"

"*That's affirmative. I'll do a visual and get back with you.*"

"*Clear. Visual only… please be careful.*"

I pulled my black clothes out of my duffle. Black sweat

jacket, black leggings, and my black combat boots. If I had to go hands on, I didn't want to do it in my chucks and sweatpants, plus those combat boots helped me pack a pretty powerful front kick. I changed quickly, pulled my hair into a tight bun, threw on my Air Force ball cap, and took off into the sky.

The clouds were low lying, providing a perfect cover for flying out. When I got closer, I flew down to the surface of the water and snuck up to the back of the Sydney Jo. The deck of the boat was dimly lit, but lights from below deck were enough that I could see inside some of the rooms. I planted my body firmly against the side of the boat and slid across. I came to the first window and peeked slowly inside. A small, but spacious bathroom decked out in black and chrome, was empty. On the counter a men's shaving kit was visible, along with an aftershave bottle. I ducked under the small porthole window and moved to the next. A bedroom, that connected to the bathroom, had a large bed that appeared to be occupied in the next porthole. I didn't look too long because I knew whoever was in that bed would see me before I saw them.

The next three were connected to a large living room and kitchen that was occupied by at least 5 men. Three were asleep on the couches and the other two sat at the kitchen table drinking out of coffee cups and talking. Apparently, they were on shifts guarding the Sydney Jo. I flew around to the other side of the boat and saw two more tiny bedrooms illuminated by a hall light, both of them empty as well.

I leaned up against the side of the boat feeling frustrated and defeated. I so much wanted Kirsten to be on the yacht. I knew wherever she was, she must be feeling so alone and scared and I wanted to help her and bring her home safely to her family.

The door opened and the two men from the kitchen came out onto the deck. They stood directly over me and I pressed myself up against the yacht as tightly as I could, holding on to a docking rope, as we rolled up and down on the waves.

They made small talk about the ocean and my island and I listened carefully to every word they said, in hopes of hearing something about Kirsten. At last, one of them gave up valuable information.

"So what happens if they don't turn over the ransom by tonight?" one asked, as my heart leapt inside of me. It started beating fast and I had to catch my breath in my excitement.

"G says we're out of here then," the other replied.

"And the girl?"

"She'll get the anchor, I guess."

I gasped, then quickly covered my mouth. It didn't take a genius to figure out what that meant. They would throw her overboard. My body started shaking at the thought of that. I had to do something quick. Kirsten had to be on this yacht somewhere.

"Speaking of that, you better go down below and check on her," one instructed the other. A lit cigarette flew over the rail and into the ocean, followed by footsteps across the deck. I watched in the shadows, as the shaggy blonde haired guy went down a flight of stairs that led below the deck. A long thin light appeared through a window I hadn't noticed before, at the bow of the yacht. In fact, it didn't even look like a window. I thought it was part of the yacht design.

I did my best to see through the blurry window and was able to make out a bed and a figure laying in it, but that's all. The blonde guy walked over to the bed and stood over her, then leaned down. My heart beat even faster, not knowing what he would do to her. He grabbed her shoulder and rolled her over, making her arm fall lifelessly off the side of the bed. The guy moved the blanket back and I knew in an instant it was Kirsten. Her long fiery red hair fell to the floor and then to my relief, he turned off the light and left.

Oh God. What should I do now? The Sydney Jo was so heavily guarded and unless I just walked in and grabbed Kirsten, there was no way I would be getting her off this yacht. Maybe I should have gone back and radioed Zhao for help, but even then I would have put her life in danger and any of the Coast Guard that showed up as well. By this time it was already four and I had just one hour of darkness left.

Shaggy blonde guy bounced up the staircase and met his buddy again.

"She's good, man. Still out of it from the hit earlier."

"Did you lock the door back?" the other guy asked.

"Yep, all secure."

They both went back into the kitchen and I sat up on the side of the deck behind a couch. I was pretty exhausted from flying for so long and needed a break.

Two obstacles now faced me. First of all, Kirsten was obviously drugged. I was going to have to fly her all the way back to the airfield, dead weight. Secondly, I had a locked door to get through with no key and nothing to use other than a kick and combat boots.

In that moment, I prayed. I prayed hard, but knew what I had to do was so obvious. I had to get Kirsten off this yacht. I thought again about Kass and how desperate I would be to save her.

I slid over to the wall by the kitchen and peeked in. No sign of the men anywhere. Just beyond the door was the staircase the blond shaggy guy had gone down. I scooted across the floor and tiptoed down the stairs. At the bottom was a door that opened easily into a small dark hallway, illuminated by a dim yellow light. I silently shut the door behind me and made my way to another door at the very end. This had to be the room, because the window was at the bow of the boat.

I slid my hand through the handle and turned it slowly, but it stopped. Just like the guy said. It was locked.

I knocked softly on the door. "Kirsten?" I whispered. No reply. I knocked a little harder. "Kirsten?" I said a little louder, but still no reply. This was the moment of truth. Was I sure I wanted to do this? Once I kicked this door in, there would be no turning back.

THIRTY-SIX

I TOOK A deep breath, knowing what I had to do. I paused for a moment like Professor Corral had taught me and closed my eyes, imagining myself kicking the door in, then made my leg the center focus of my thoughts. I stepped back, shifted my feet, did a back step and side kicked the door. To my delight, the hollow door busted to pieces, which was great, but also made a loud shattering noise that pierced the quiet night.

Kirsten laid still on the bed, not moving a muscle, in spite of all the commotion. I leaned over her listening for some sign of life. She was barely responsive and her breathing, extremely shallow. Her skin was pale and cold in the freezing room.

"Kirsten?" I said tapping on her cheeks in an attempt to wake her. "Kirsten, wake up."

For a moment, her eyes opened and she looked up at me. There was no reaction, just a blank stare before she closed them again. She looked so innocent and much too young to be here.

"Alright sweetie," I whispered, "let's get you out of here."

I picked her up, cradling her in my arms. She was just a bit smaller than me, so this was quite the challenge. I was just getting ready to step over the broken door, when a chilling voice echoed through my body.

"Bad news, sweetheart. Silent alarm," the shaggy blonde guy smirked, standing at the end of the hallway.

I gasped, backing slowly into the room and set Kirsten back on the bed, never taking my eyes off the guy.

"Who are you here with?" he yelled, coming towards me, a shiny pocket knife in his hand.

I backed up further, my eyes wide with fear, but very quickly that fear turned to anger. Faces of my family and friends, Johnny and Zhao, flashed through my thoughts and something inside of me snapped. I immediately went into defense mode as he turned me around, grabbing around my neck with his arm and squeezing the blade of the knife, slicing the jaw line of my face. The blood rushed to my head and for a moment I felt like I would pass out. I realized by his grip, that he had no training in martial arts and that helped me relax and revert to all my training. I had been choked out so many times by skilled people, I knew he had no chance against me. I remembered Professor B's words, to "address the grip".

I immediately buried my chin to my chest to ease the pressure off of my neck and grabbed his left hand that held the knife, moving it away from my face. I dropped my weight going into a crouch, pulling his weight slightly onto my back, as I grabbed his right arm that was around my neck with my right hand. I hip tossed him to the ground in front of me by kneeling down to my left knee. He landed hard, further showing his lack of training. The knife slid from his hand landing a few feet from him. I kept my grip on his right arm and stepped over his head with one leg and his chest with my other and sat to my bottom. Instead of politely and slowly locking his arm out, like I was trained to while rolling with friends, I popped my hips with all of my energy, then heard a sickening crack from his arm, followed by his painful scream. He was making so much noise, I knew I had to get out fast. I jumped up quickly and was just about to pick up Kirsten again, when I heard more footsteps coming down the stairs.

"Finn?" the deep voice called down.

Finn continued to thrash around unable to say anything coherent.

"Finn?" the voice called out again.

What should I do now? This guy on the floor wasn't much of a challenge, but I had seen the other guy on the deck and he was a brute. He had numerous scars and his ears looked like they had seen better days, revealing that he had trained or at least had his share of fights over the years. With all my energy spent on flying, I didn't know how well I'd fare with him. Then I remembered my pepper spray Johnny had given me. Leaving it for now in my pocket, I silently moved to the side of the door and waited for him to enter.

I saw the gun first. He had it out in front of him as he entered the room. His hand was shaking, likely after seeing Finn writhing on the ground with a broken arm. This guy was as scared as I was. He stepped through the door, gun out in front in his right hand, using his left to push what was left of the door jam out of the way of his large frame. I saw my chance and stepped under his gun hand, gripping his sleeve with my right hand with my back to him. Using my right shoulder for a fulcrum under his gun arm, I stomped his right foot with the heel of my Danner boot, keeping it on the ground, while I pulled his hand with both of mine down towards my stomach. Of course arms don't bend the way, but I'm not ashamed to say that his did after that. His deep guttural growl told me his arm was no longer in play as the gun fell from his now useless hand. I turned into him and struck him along the angle of his jaw with my left forearm stunning him slightly. I stepped through leaving my right leg behind his right and hip tossed him pretty effortlessly to the ground as his balance was interrupted by his broken arm and the distracting strike to his jaw. He landed a bit better than Finn showing at least some knowledge of the proper technique. I then pulled the pepper spray from my pocket and hit him with a solid spray to the face.He didn't like how that felt and raged, yelling colorful profanities towards me. I side kicked him, catching him just below his nose, hoping for enough time to get Kirsten moving and out of there. I caught a quick whiff of the spray and relaxed, thankful I'd been trained to work through its effects.

"Thank you Professor B," I said under my breath.

I ran to Kirsten and struggled picking her up, already tired from my long flight and fighting these losers. I made it with her down the hall and up the stairs.

"There!" I heard a voice behind me yell when I cleared the final step.

I jumped up onto the deck and just before we lifted off, two more men came running in our direction. The one was right up on us, as I shot off the deck. I looked down at three sets of stunned wide eyes, staring at us take off. No matter how many times I've seen it, watching people's faces as they see me fly off never gets old. This time was particularly satisfying and in my anger toward them, I did the only thing I could do with my arms and hands full. I smirked and stuck my tongue out. Childish I know, but oh so satisfying.

I flew straight up above the yacht, getting us safely behind the clouds, then over to my rock on the island. I didn't want to stay here too long, because I was pretty positive this would be the first place they would come to look for us, once they got over their initial shock. At the same time I was exhausted and needed a moment to rest before the flight home. It would take all the energy I had left. I looked at my Saturn ring tattoo, that was now a dull pink, reminding me of my energy depletion.

I set Kirsten down on my sleeping bag and grabbed my radio. I didn't even bother to click it.

"*Flygirl to Zhao...umm Kyoto. Flygirl to Kyoto. Do you copy?*" I knew I sounded desperate, but I was feeling desperate. Kirsten was not doing well. I knew she needed some Narcan and fast.

"*Kyoto here!*" Zhao answered instantly. "*FLYGIRL?! WHERE HAVE YOU BEEN?!*"

Yikes. He was mad.

"*Kyoto I've got her. I'll be leaving here in 10 minutes and I need you to meet me at the airstrip in 30 minutes. She needs medical attention fast. Do you copy? 30 minutes!*"

"*What!? You have her?!*" he almost screamed at me.

"*Affirmative,*" I answered as calmly as I could.

"*Flygirl...how?!*" he yelled at me

"*Just meet me there!*" I yelled back, all of our radio etiquette flying right out the window.

"*Fine! Fine!*" he answered, clearly annoyed.

I sighed and rolled my eyes, hooking up my headphones to my radio so I could talk to Zhao hands free, mid-flight if I needed to. All my stuff would have to stay here, since there was no way I could carry it with Kirsten. I had to hurry and pack it, though. The sun would be rising in 30 minutes, but if I could just stay above the cloud line, there was a good chance I could avoid being seen.

A cool breeze enveloped me and it was then that I noticed my sticky, wet neck. I touched my hand to my face, my fingers tinted by my vibrant pink and red blood. That jerk must have cut me good. My adrenaline had been pumping so hard, I had barely noticed.

I threw my packed duffle bag into the brush, my ribs throbbing now from the fight. I took the bandage wrap I had kept out and wrapped them as fast as I could, along with my jaw to try and slow down the bleeding. Next, I picked up Kirsten and secured her with the makeshift parachute cords Zhao had found last minute. It wasn't the most secure, but it was better than nothing.

"Ok Kirsten," I said. "Let's get you home.

THIRTY-SEVEN

TEN MINUTES INTO flight, I could feel my arms getting numb and I still had another thirty to go. I cradled Kirsten tightly, not flying as fast as I could, out of fear I would drop her.

To be safe, I decided to find a place to rest for a moment and flew down below the cloud line. No land was in sight, but luckily a long merchant ship was sailing nearby. I landed down at the very end of the ship and hid among the shipment crates, then turned on my radio.

"*Flygirl to Kyoto.*"

"*Go ahead Flygirl.*"

"*I'm twenty minutes away. I stopped for a 5.*"

"*Clear. I'm almost to Dillingham. I'll meet you at rendezvous D-5.*"

"*Clear.*"

I was so excited to almost be there, but paused for a moment to catch my breath. I was exhausted, but knew I had to get back in the air, this ship was starting to take me way off course.

I scooped Kirsten up and gently lifted us off the crate, as the sun began to rise in the east. Her weight shifted in my arms, prompting me to look down at her. To my relief, her big blue eyes stared back at me. She looked around and began fidgeting when she realized where she was.

"Kirsten, stay still. Do you understand me? Everything will be explained to you when we land. Everything's ok. I got you and I'm not letting go."

"Claire?" she asked in astonishment.

"Yes."

Luckily she closed her eyes, but luck wasn't completely on my side. Little did Zhao and I know the Coast Guard had overheard all of our radio transmissions and they, along with the special forces, and a host of firetrucks and ambulances would be awaiting our arrival at Dillingham. Their assumption being that I was a small, unknown plane in distress, with a patient in trouble on board.

Zhao arrived at the airfield first and parked his car at the end of the runway. He breathed a sigh of relief to find no one around, but grew anxious with the sun rising. At least the clouds were thick and low. He instructed me via the radio to stay in the clouds until just above the air field, then drop straight down at the furthest end of the runway.

We didn't have a chance of that happening, though. I was coming in heavy. My arms were ready to give out and I had to land fast before I lost Kirsten.

Zhao would later tell me what happened. Everything was quiet as he searched the sky for any sign of me, then suddenly they all charged the runway like a mighty army. First the ambulances and firetrucks, sirens screaming, and Zhao assuming they were headed to something on the other side of the airfield. But they rushed toward our runway while two Coast Guard boats appeared in the distance, making a beeline towards the airfield.

"Flygirl from Kyoto, abort! Abort!" he yelled on the radio, but it was too late. I was already breaking through the clouds. I had no choice, but to land with Kirsten. We were both freezing in the dewey clouds and her breathing was not getting better. She needed medical attention immediately and I refused to let all I did to save her be in vain.

I looked down to see a couple of dozen people, all decked out in their first responder uniforms looking up at the sky expecting a plane to appear. Their faces turned to fright and they began yelling to one another in chaos, when they realized what they were witnessing. Some of them took out their phone and videoed or took pictures with the flashes popping all around. Others ran and hid in the trucks in fright.

I held onto Kirsten tighter and buried my face behind

her, but that didn't do much good. We landed close to the end of the runway and I froze with her still in my arms. For a quiet moment we all stood looking at each other.

Zhao ran to me and quickly unraveled Kirsten from the cords. "Run Claire," he whispered. "Go to the beach. I'll find you." He then turned to take her to an ambulance. "Someone help! This girl needs help!" I heard him yell behind me, as I took off running to the beach.

A barrier stood at the end of the runway, just 200 feet away. If I could just get to the barrier and jump over it, I could make it down to the beach and disappear. I ran with all my might, which I didn't have much left of. My ribs throbbed, now that the adrenaline in my body had worn down. I was almost there, when out of nowhere a black SUV rolled up beside me. I looked over at the SUV, my eyes full of fear and ran even harder.

"Claire!" a voice yelled out. "Stop!" But I refused, keeping my eyes focused on the barrier that was so close.

In an instant, the door to the SUV opened and a strong arm came out, wrapping around me. I was sucked into the SUV as we did a 180 and sped out of the back gate of Dillingham. I caught my breath and looked around me.

"Mr. Lucas?" I said in shock.

"Yes," he answered. "Lt. General Gray sent me. Man girl, when you said you were worth all the trouble you were right."

I nodded in agreement with him. "I can fly, Mr. Lucas."

"Yeah," he smiled, shaking his head. "I know and now...now the whole world knows too."

THE END

About the Author

Cynthia L. McDaniel is a Clarksville, Tennessee native, who resides in Northwest Indiana. When not writing, she enjoys spending time with her family, running, swimming in the Ocean, and vacations to anywhere that involves a beach. *New Heights* is Cynthia's second novel in the Sky Walker series and she looks forward to publishing the third and final one.

Cynthia loves to connect with her readers and other authors, and you can find her on Goodreads, on Facebook @CynthiaLMcDanielauthor, on Instagram @cynthialmcdanielauthor, or on Twitter @CynthiaLMcDani2.

Hi There!

Thank you so much for reading *New Heights*! I hope you enjoyed it! I have one more book in this series coming in 2021, so if you've enjoyed following the adventures of Claire stay tuned!

If you would like, you can go to Amazon and leave a review. Reviews help Indie authors like me tremendously.

I enjoy hearing from my readers, so please contact me if you have any questions or would just like to chat!

XOXO,

Cynthia

www.ingramcontent.com/pod-product-compliance
Lightning Source LLC
Chambersburg PA
CBHW052022240626
47153CB00006B/1909